THE BLACK HORIZON

BY

Uno Nguyen

ISBN: 9798301536496

Table of Contents

THE SHATTERED VANGUARD

Davros Phaedrus stood in the sterile corridor, his heavy boots making no sound against the metallic flooring of the Rubicon Spire. A fortress of cold metal and circuitry, the Spire loomed like a twisted monument to both technology and flesh, orbiting the shattered remnants of a planet long forgotten. The station was a place where soldiers went to die—or, worse yet, to be transformed into something unrecognizable. And as a disgraced former Deathwatch marine, Davros had been dispatched here not out of duty, but as a reminder of his failures. His honor, his reputation—both had been shattered on a mission that ended in blood and the screams of his brothers. Now, he was a mere shadow of his former self, entrusted with a task that seemed more fitting for a monster than a soldier.

He pulled himself to attention as the doors to the laboratory hissed open. Beyond them, the cold glow of surgical lights illuminated a nightmare—a place where science and suffering intertwined in unspeakable ways. The lab smelled faintly of antiseptic, but there was something beneath it—something darker. The acrid scent of burning flesh. The unmistakable tang of blood.

Inside, he found the subject awaiting his procedure—a man, once a sergeant in the Imperial Guard, now stripped to his bare skin, his eyes wide with terror. Sergeant Gael's once-muscular frame was now little more than a cadaver in waiting, covered in scars, tattoos, and veins bulging with the toxic concoction that had been injected into his bloodstream. The surgical table where he lay was adorned with strange, mechanical contraptions—needles, drills, and serrated blades—designed to break the human body down and rebuild it as something far more sinister.

Davros could hear the muffled whispers of the medical staff in the background, their voices clinical, detached, as if this was just another procedure. To them, it was. To Davros, it felt like the violation of something sacred.

"Ready the subject," came the command, cold and emotionless. Davros nodded, stepping forward reluctantly. This was his charge now—to supervise the high-risk Rubicon Surgery. The procedure, meant to transform men into living war machines, was seen as a necessary evil. A weapon for those desperate enough to embrace it. Yet, as Davros stared down at Gael's trembling form, he felt the first stirrings of doubt.

The room's lighting flickered for a moment, casting long shadows across the walls. Gael's chest heaved, his breath coming in shallow gasps as the cybernetic arms of the surgery station lowered into place, locking onto his limbs with mechanical precision. Davros had seen this before—he had witnessed the horrors of Rubicon Surgery on countless other soldiers, but this time felt different. The sterile atmosphere, the machinery, the sharp tang of blood—it all seemed so wrong.

With a sudden, painful screech, the drill began its work. Gael's back arched in agony, and his eyes bulged as the massive needle pressed deep into his spine. The sound was sickening—a mix of bone grinding and flesh stretching unnaturally. The blood spurted in fat, red globs, staining the table and pooling on the floor. His body twitched violently as the machines hummed, fusing metal into his skin. A horrific, mechanical noise filled the room, as if the world itself was rejecting the procedure.

"Hold him steady," a voice barked from behind Davros, snapping him from his horrified stupor. He quickly stepped back, but his eyes stayed locked on the nightmare unfolding before him. Gael's body trembled as the machine continued its work, but something was wrong—far more wrong than usual.

The sergeant's flesh began to bubble, the skin pulling away from his muscles in great, wet sheets. His body spasmed uncontrollably as the cybernetic enhancements integrated with his flesh, but instead of becoming stronger, he became something worse. Something monstrous. The seams where metal met skin began to split, tearing open like a hideous flower in bloom. Gael's body was mutating—grotesque, contorted. A jagged, steel limb shot out from his shoulder, followed by another from his chest. His eyes rolled back, a sickening scream tearing from his throat as the metal and flesh fused in ways that defied logic.

The transformation escalated rapidly, as if the body was rejecting the procedure. Gael's muscles and bones snapped, twisting in ways no human form should. Blood poured in torrents as his insides rearranged themselves, spilling out from gaping wounds. His screams, muffled and gargled, were almost drowned out by the shrieking, grinding metal that surrounded him.

Then, with a final, terrible convulsion, the sergeant's body gave out entirely. His chest split open with a sickening sound, spilling organs and wires onto the floor. But even in death, Gael was not quiet. His mouth opened in a final, grotesque howl, only to fall silent as the last vestiges of life drained from his form. The result of the surgery—an unnatural, malformed creature—lay crumpled and twitching on the table, its limbs splayed in impossible directions.

The room fell into an eerie silence, broken only by the soft hum of machinery. Davros stared, his stomach churning, unable to look away. He had seen this before, but never like this. Never so close. Gael's body had failed to survive the procedure, but it was still… something. A thing caught between man and machine. A mockery of both.

The others in the room moved forward, but Davros could barely keep his feet steady. The surgeon in charge nodded grimly, already preparing to discard the creature's remains. But before he could turn away, something strange happened.

From the grotesque corpse, a faint whispering sound emerged—soft, barely audible. At first, Davros thought it was the wind. But no, it came from Gael's mouth, a rasping hiss that chilled his spine.

"You'll join us… soon…" the voice croaked, distorted and broken, as if the creature still retained some semblance of the man it had once been.

The words were a death sentence, a prophecy. But to Davros, they felt more like a warning.

Davros couldn't shake the image of Gael's mangled body. His mind recoiled, yet he found himself drawn deeper into the bowels of Rubicon Spire, as though some unseen force was compelling him to understand the madness that had infected the station. The cold, metallic walls of the upper levels gave way to darker, more oppressive corridors. The lights flickered above him as he descended, the flicker casting long, unholy shadows across the walls. The air here was thick, stagnant—almost alive with the tension of something waiting to break free.

Every step seemed to echo in the silence, but it wasn't the kind of silence that brought comfort. No, this silence was heavy, suffocating. The deeper he went, the more the station felt like a tomb, and the more he was aware of the unnatural stillness that clung to the place like a curse. It wasn't just the dead soldiers that haunted these halls—it was something worse. Something unseen. The Warp.

He passed rooms filled with grotesque, mutated figures— soldiers whose bodies had been twisted and warped beyond recognition. Some were little more than moving, decaying husks, their limbs fused with steel and flesh in horrific ways. Their faces were frozen in expressions of agony or madness. Some were barely alive, begging for death in strained voices, while others had long since lost their humanity, speaking only in garbled, mechanical phrases, their minds eroded by the surgeries.

"Help me… please…" one of them rasped as Davros passed. It was a soldier, his face obscured by jagged metal, but the eyes—those eyes… They were still human. Pleading. It was a moment of sheer vulnerability, and it struck Davros harder than he could have imagined. How long had this man been in agony? How many others had been subjected to the same fate?

He turned a corner and found himself before a large, reinforced door. The nameplate read "Dr. Celeste Thorn—Research and Development." His gut twisted at the thought of entering. He had heard whispers about her—the mind behind Rubicon Surgery. It was said that she was brilliant, but brilliant minds were often the most dangerous.

With a hiss, the door slid open.

Inside, Dr. Celeste Thorn stood hunched over a table, her delicate fingers moving with meticulous precision. The sharp smell of chemicals filled the air, and a soft hum came from the array of equipment she was using. Her lab coat was pristine, despite the gruesome nature of the work being carried out just a few rooms away. She looked up as Davros entered, her cold, calculating gaze locking onto him with an unsettling intensity.

"Major Phaedrus, I presume?" Her voice was smooth, almost too smooth, like silk slipping over skin.

"I've seen the horrors in the lower levels," Davros said, his voice tight with disgust. "What is this place really?"

Dr. Thorn's lips curled into a faint, almost imperceptible smile. "What you see is merely the next step in the evolution of warfare. Humanity has always sought to improve itself. To evolve beyond its limitations. The Rubicon Spire is where that dream becomes a reality." She gestured to the room around her, the walls adorned with holographic displays of soldier enhancements, military tactics, and diagnostic readouts.

"And what of the… people?" Davros asked, his throat dry. "The soldiers—are they… human?"

"Of course they are," she replied, her voice betraying no emotion. "They are more human than ever. Our work is about merging the best of man with the best of machine. The boundaries between flesh and metal are irrelevant. We can make soldiers invincible, unstoppable. Perfect."

Davros wanted to protest, wanted to scream at her, but the words stuck in his throat. He had seen the results of their 'perfection,' and it was monstrous.

Before he could speak, a low growl echoed from the far corner of the room, followed by the sound of metal scraping against metal. Davros turned sharply to see a figure—no, a thing— struggling against its restraints. Its body was a twisted mass of flesh and steel, the sinews of its arms barely holding the mangled form together. The figure was twitching uncontrollably, its eyes wild and bloodshot, as it strained against the chains that bound it to the wall.

"What is that?" Davros demanded, stepping back, his hand instinctively reaching for the weapon at his side.

Dr. Thorn remained calm, almost indifferent. "One of our most recent failures. Subject 217. It's… unstable."

The creature's roar was deafening as it tore free of its restraints, sending them clattering to the floor. It surged forward, its body spasming as it struggled to stand. Its mouth opened wide, revealing rows of jagged, steel teeth, as it lunged at Davros, its grotesque body moving with unnatural speed.

The room exploded into chaos. Davros barely managed to duck as the creature hurtled toward him, its claws slashing through the air. He felt the breeze of its passing, the stench of its rotting flesh filling his nostrils. In one swift motion, he drew his sidearm and fired, the shot hitting the creature square in the chest. It didn't stop—it didn't even flinch. The creature snarled and lunged again, but this time, Davros was ready. He dived to the side, narrowly avoiding its jaws as they snapped shut, missing his throat by mere inches.

"Contain it!" Dr. Thorn shouted, her voice clinical even in the face of imminent death.

Davros scrambled to his feet, his heart racing. He fired another round, but the creature was relentless. It crashed into a table, sending equipment flying in all directions. The room became a blur of frantic motion, screams, and the sound of flesh tearing. The creature finally collapsed, its body twitching as the last of its life drained away. The blood-soaked room was silent, save for the ragged breathing of Davros.

Dr. Thorn walked over, her expression unchanged, even as the blood of her failed experiment stained the floor. She glanced at the remains of the creature with a detached air, almost admiring it. "This… this is progress," she murmured, as though the blood-soaked aftermath was just another minor inconvenience. "These are merely growing pains, Major."

Davros, heart pounding, stared at her in disbelief. How could she be so calm? So detached?

Endline: As Thorn watched the blood-soaked aftermath, she smiled coldly: "These are merely growing pains, Major."

The deeper Davros descended into Rubicon Spire, the more the station seemed to warp around him. At first, it was subtle—a flicker at the edge of his vision, a low hum beneath the constant mechanical drone of the facility. But the whispers… they began as faint murmurs, just below the threshold of comprehension. He dismissed them at first, chalking it up to the stress of his assignment, to the madness of the place. Yet, with each step, they grew louder, more distinct.

"Davros... Phaedrus..."

His name, like a chant, a twisted litany echoing from all directions. His augmented senses, already honed to razor precision by his Deathwatch training, were becoming unnervingly sensitive to these sounds. The air around him seemed to thrum with an unnatural energy, as if something was watching, listening, waiting for him to unravel.

The aches in his body were the first warning signs. His implants, which had always been reliable, were beginning to throb. His spine seemed to grind with each step, the joints in his arms and legs whined as if protesting the heavy weight of his cybernetic enhancements. He felt the cold crawl of something insidious beneath his skin. It was like the very metal of his body was rejecting him. It felt as though some force, dark and invasive, was crawling under his flesh, threading its way through his bones and nerves.

He tried to push through it, to ignore the physical torment and the growing voice that seemed to echo in his mind. But the whispers were relentless.

"More... must take... all..."

They had become a maddening chant. He felt himself losing focus, his mind lurching as though it, too, was beginning to warp under the pressure. It was as though something was inside of him, prodding, nudging, pushing him to open the doors of the Rubicon Spire even further.

That's when he found it.

At the heart of the Spire was a hidden level—a place that didn't appear on any schematics, a place deeper than any military-grade security protocol. It was here that Davros stumbled upon the true horror of the Rubicon Corporation. The room was cold, filled with rows of tanks. But these weren't the standard incubation or regeneration chambers used to treat soldiers. These were grotesque, horrifying. Inside each of the transparent containers were soldiers, but not in any form he recognized. They were suspended in viscous fluid, their bodies twitching involuntarily as mechanical limbs fused grotesquely with their flesh. Some were barely alive—parts of them were no longer human, twisted beyond recognition.

But what was worse was the sound. Each tank emitted a low, rhythmic hum, and as Davros approached, he saw the soldiers' eyes—if they could still be called eyes—staring blankly forward, unblinking. Some of them whispered, but their voices were garbled, mangled beyond the point of speech, their mouths contorted in unnatural angles. A few were even murmuring his name—his own name—like an ancient prayer that only he could hear.

He stumbled backward, his breath coming in shallow gasps. His mind was starting to fracture, the whispers growing louder still. His vision blurred, and the walls seemed to pulse, as though the Spire itself was alive, feeding off the suffering of the soldiers it had created.

A flickering monitor caught his eye. It was displaying a series of data feeds, but it was the text at the bottom of the screen that caused his heart to seize in his chest.

Project Prometheus: Phase 7—Necron Integration Complete. Warp Energies Engaged. Initiating Mind-Link Integration.

The words were a chilling revelation. Davros knew the implications immediately. The Rubicon Corporation, in its quest to 'enhance' humanity, had begun experimenting with the forbidden—Warp-tainted Necron technology. The machines of the Necrons, already imbued with terrible power, had been fused with the very energies of the Warp itself, creating an unholy hybrid of metal, flesh, and the unnatural. And these poor soldiers—these victims—had been the test subjects.

A small part of him tried to deny it. But the evidence was right there, staring back at him. The fusion of ancient Necron tech with Warp energies had created something even more terrifying: soldiers who could never die. A perverse immortality—though one twisted by agony, madness, and mechanical monstrosity.

Davros' pulse quickened as his eyes scanned the screen. A list of names scrolled past, each one marked with an ominous red tag, indicating they had been selected for the next stage. His breath caught in his throat as he saw it. His name was at the top of the list.

He stumbled back, a cold sweat breaking out over his skin. His mind screamed in protest, but it was too late. His body was already a part of their plan. The Rubicon Corporation had no intention of letting him leave—he was nothing more than another tool to be corrupted, another soldier to be dissected and remade in their image.

As the whispers reached a crescendo, drowning out all rational thought, Davros could only whisper to himself in a hollow, desperate voice.

"This isn't enhancement… it's damnation."

He was already lost.

The drop pods slammed into the crumbling soil of the planet's surface with an ear-shattering impact. Davros barely registered the explosion of dust and debris as the door of his pod opened. His body—already augmented with Deathwatch protocols—moved with practiced precision, his boots sinking slightly into the ash-choked ground as he hit the battlefield. The world was a wasteland, a dying, scorched rock that had once known the touch of life. But now, only death lingered.

This mission was supposed to be simple. Retrieve the Aeldari artefact and return. That was all. But Davros knew that there was no such thing as a simple mission anymore, not after what he'd seen aboard Rubicon Spire. The whispers, the madness—he could feel it all closing in on him like a tightening noose.

His squad—six other seasoned warriors—moved in tight formation, weapons raised, their steps heavy on the ashen earth. The sky was the color of blood, streaked with the dying light of a distant star. The air was thick with the stench of decay. As they moved through the charred remnants of what had once been a great city,

Davros couldn't shake the feeling that they were being watched. The Aeldari were known for their trickery, their ability to strike from the shadows. But this—this felt different.

The ground trembled beneath their feet, and then, from the smoke-shrouded horizon, the first of the Aeldari appeared. They were like ghosts, their lithe forms moving with an almost unnatural grace. Their armor shimmered in the red light, their weapons glowing with an eerie energy. They came not with a roar, but with a deadly silence, their blades flashing like the flicker of a dying flame.

The first ambush hit like a storm. In an instant, the battlefield erupted in chaos. Davros spun, raising his boltgun, firing into the advancing Aeldari. His squad responded in kind, but their shots seemed to pass through the ethereal forms of their enemies, who dodged and weaved with impossible agility.

The sound of plasma fire and gunshots filled the air, but there was something else—a deep, pulsing hum beneath the violence, as if the very fabric of reality was beginning to bend. The whispers returned, louder now, screaming at him from all directions, from within his mind.

"Davros… Davros… you cannot escape us…"

He gritted his teeth and pushed forward, eyes scanning the battlefield, seeking the artefact that Rubicon had sent him to retrieve. It was supposed to be a simple objective: a small, alien relic buried deep in the ruins of this forsaken city. But as he moved, the battlefield twisted and shifted around him. The Aeldari were relentless, but it was the other forces, the unseen ones, that chilled him to his core.

Davros' augmented vision began to distort. His internal sensors, already flickering, malfunctioned as the Warp energy began to bleed through. His flesh twitched, crawling beneath his armor. The metal limbs, the cybernetic enhancements he'd come to rely on, began to ache as though they were alive, rejecting their place in his body. His skin burned and bubbled. He could feel it—something inside him, something *wrong*—as the Warp's influence seeped deeper into his bones.

A comrade screamed beside him as his arm was severed in a spray of blood. The warrior crumpled to the ground in a heap, his body twitching unnaturally as his other arm flailed, still holding his weapon. Davros didn't have time to mourn. The Aeldari were upon them, their energy blades cutting through his comrades like a hot knife through flesh. Each step forward felt like wading through tar. His movements slowed. The whispers grew louder, more frantic, until they were a cacophony of madness in his mind.

"Embrace the change…" one voice purred, "Be one with the machine… you are beyond flesh."

As Davros pressed on, the landscape around him seemed to distort, as though reality itself were breaking apart. He turned a corner into an ancient, half-collapsed temple—its dark spires rising like twisted fingers into the blood-red sky. In the center of the ruins lay the artefact.

It was a small, unassuming object, a glowing shard encased in an intricate web of runes. But as Davros approached, the air grew thick with a palpable, malignant energy. The artefact pulsed with a sickly green light, as though it were alive, its energy warping the space around it. The whispers swirled louder, now clearly speaking in tongues, their voices indistinct, alien, echoing in his skull.

In the reflection of the artefact's smooth surface, Davros saw himself—a twisted, grotesque version of himself. His face was partly obscured by jagged metal, his eyes glowing with unnatural intensity. His body, once a pristine example of Deathwatch enhancements, was now something monstrous—part human, part machine, twisted by the Warp's influence. The sight was a horror, a vision of the future he dreaded most. His own reflection screamed at him, its voice a distorted, mechanical rasp.

"No… no, this can't be real…" he muttered to himself, his hand reaching toward the artefact, drawn to it despite the overwhelming sense of dread that filled him.

Uno Nguyen © 2024

As his fingers touched the surface of the artefact, the world seemed to rip apart. The ground shuddered violently beneath his feet, and an ear-splitting wail erupted from the skies above. A cold, unbearable chill ran through his body as the voices in his head reached a fever pitch.

"You are already ours…"

The words didn't come from the artefact. They came from within him, within his very soul. The artefact was not just an object—it was a gateway, a conduit to something far darker. The Warp, the Aeldari, Rubicon Corporation—it was all part of the same damnation.

His fingers clenched around the artefact, the metal burning into his skin. His body convulsed as the alien energies surged through him, melding with the machinery that had already corrupted his flesh. His vision blurred as his mind fractured, pieces of his humanity slipping away like grains of sand.

Davros staggered back onto the cold metal surface of the Rubicon Spire, his mind still reeling from the horrors of the battlefield. The artefact, now secured in his grip, pulsed ominously in the darkened corridors as he made his way back to the labs. His enhanced senses screamed at him—something was terribly wrong. The atmosphere was charged with a sickening energy that crawled under his skin, the Warp's influence seeping deeper into the very walls of the station. The whispers were louder now, like a distant storm on the horizon, ready to devour everything in its path.

"Thorn... you have no idea what you've done," he muttered under his breath, his voice hollow, a grim echo of the man he once was.

Upon reaching the lab complex, Davros found the doors to Dr. Celeste Thorn's office open. Inside, Thorn was standing before a massive holo-table, studying the readings from the artefact. Her expression remained cool and detached, as if the entire nightmare they were about to unleash was nothing more than a scientific curiosity.

Davros stepped inside, his fist clenched around the Necron artefact. His breath was heavy, his body trembling with a mix of exhaustion and mounting rage.

"Thorn!" he shouted, his voice raw with the weight of his discovery. "What is this? What have you done?"

Thorn turned to him slowly, her eyes cold and calculating. There was no shock on her face, no sign of guilt or fear. Just a detached professionalism.

"I did what was necessary, Major Phaedrus," she replied, her voice smooth as silk. "The Rubicon Surgery is meant to advance humanity, to push beyond the limitations of flesh and bone. This artefact—" She gestured to the glowing shard in his hand. "—is the key to unlocking the next phase of human evolution. We've barely scratched the surface of its power."

Davros's heart thudded painfully in his chest. "You're insane. That thing—it's a Necron device. The Warp's energy is—" He struggled to find the words. The realization was too much. "It's tearing apart everything around us! You've unleashed something that will destroy us all."

Thorn's lips curled into a cold smile. "You still don't understand, do you? This is *progress*. It's not about humanity anymore. It's about ascension, becoming more than what we were. The Warp is a tool, nothing more. And this artefact... it's the key to our *evolution*."

Davros felt the bile rise in his throat. His body was on fire with the horrible realization. She wasn't just a scientist. She was a zealot—an architect of his damnation.

Before he could respond, the room shook violently. The lights flickered, casting long, twisted shadows against the walls. The

Uno Nguyen © 2024

station groaned under the pressure, its systems malfunctioning one after another.

Then came the screaming.

Davros's heart sank as the comms crackled to life. "The experiment... it's gone... *wrong*!" the panicked voice of a technician blurted out over the intercom. "The *creations*... they're—"

A deafening crash erupted from down the hallway, followed by the horrible sound of twisted metal grinding against bone. Davros's instincts kicked in. He sprinted down the hallway, Thorn close behind him, her heels clicking eerily in the madness.

What he saw next would haunt him for the rest of his life.

In the lab ahead, soldiers—once human—were slaughtering one another. Their bodies, once augmented, were now grotesque, twisting mass of flesh and machinery. Some had limbs that stretched impossibly long, while others were barely recognizable, their faces contorted into horrific masks of metal and bone. These were the very soldiers who had once served the Imperium, twisted beyond recognition by the horrific experiments sanctioned by Rubicon. And now, they were tearing through everything in their path.

Davros watched in stunned horror as one of the soldiers—a hulking figure with limbs that seemed to stretch like rubber—swung a jagged, serrated blade through the chest of another soldier. The other soldier fell to the floor, his body contorting unnaturally before he was consumed in a chaotic spray of blood and sparks.

"Thorn! We need to get out of here!" Davros shouted over the chaos, but she seemed unfazed. Instead, her eyes gleamed with a mixture of cold excitement and scientific curiosity.

"No, Major," she said, her voice calm, "This is what we've been waiting for. This is evolution."

Davros didn't have time to argue. As a mutated soldier lunged at him, he raised his bolter, blasting it to pieces. But the sound of gunfire only seemed to further enrage the creatures around him. They were drawn to the noise, hungry for destruction.

He turned to see a monstrous figure charging toward him—a soldier whose flesh had been grotesquely stretched with metallic limbs, the joints clicking like the gears of a broken clock. Its eyes were wide, manic with rage as it crawled on all fours, the screech of metal on bone filling the air.

"Die!" Davros roared as he fired into its chest, but the thing only howled, ignoring the damage as its metal arms crashed toward him with impossible speed.

In the next instant, the creature was on him, its hands grasping his neck, pulling him toward its maw, where jagged metal teeth awaited. Davros struggled, gasping for air, as the thing's hand closed around his throat like a vice.

But as he fought for his life, he heard the cold, calculated voice of Dr. Thorn over the intercom, cutting through the madness:

"Welcome to the next stage of evolution."

BENEATH THE SKIN

Davros stood in the sterile corridors of the Rubicon Spire, his mind swirling with horrors from both the past and present. The artefact, still pulsing softly in the pack on his back, felt like a weight pressing into his very soul. The whispers had become louder, more insistent, echoing through the back of his mind as he slept. Every night, the same nightmare—visions of a Necron Tomb World awakening beneath the surface of a forgotten planet, the ancient machines stirring to life, their eyes glowing with cold, mechanical purpose. In the nightmare, he was trapped in the tomb with the rest of his squad, his flesh being consumed by the same horrors he had witnessed in the Spire's laboratories.

It was only a matter of time before it bled into reality.

The strange, unrelenting pressure in his chest had grown unbearable. Something inside of him was changing. His enhanced body—a perfect amalgamation of man and machine—was starting to ache in ways it had never before. It felt like his flesh was rejecting the cybernetic implants, as if the artefact were somehow influencing his very biology.

"Major Phaedrus," a voice broke through his thoughts. It was Captain Leena Darron, a hard-eyed officer who had been assigned to accompany him on this new mission. Her expression was stern, but there was an underlying tension in her eyes. She handed him a data slate with a holo-map of the colony world.

"We've received orders from Command. A recently unearthed Necron tomb on a remote planet in the Sicaris system needs immediate investigation. You and your team are to head there, assess the situation, and retrieve any data that might assist Rubicon's operations. We have reason to believe the tomb could be linked to the artefact."

Davros glanced down at the slate, his blood running cold. "A Necron tomb? How long has it been unearthed?"

Darron's face was grave. "Long enough for the first wave of excavation teams to go silent. That's why you're going in. We're not sure what's happening down there, but the reports have been... unsettling."

Davros didn't respond immediately. His mind raced, torn between the growing dread of what lay beneath the planet's surface and the gnawing sense that he was already far too deep into something he couldn't escape. His fingers clenched the edges of the slate, the sharp pain bringing him back to the present.

"We'll depart immediately," he said, his voice colder than he intended.

The descent into the tomb was unlike anything Davros had experienced. The surface of the remote colony world was barren, windswept, with only a few scattered ruins marking the planet's long-abandoned history. His team—six soldiers from the Deathwatch, all hardened veterans—landed in their drop pods, the engines screaming as they cut through the atmosphere, the sound a hollow scream in the dead air.

The tomb's entrance was hidden beneath the craggy rock face of a mountain, its entrance nothing more than a dark slit in the earth, barely visible from the surface. Once they landed, the air seemed to change. The ground beneath their boots trembled with an unnatural pulse, and as they entered the darkness, the temperature dropped sharply.

The walls of the tomb stretched endlessly upward, and the air inside was thick with dust, the silence broken only by the soft echo of their boots on the cold stone. The further they ventured, the more oppressive the atmosphere became, like something ancient and malevolent was watching, waiting for them to make the first move.

"Keep your eyes peeled," Davros commanded, his voice low. "We don't know what we're walking into."

As they advanced, the walls of the tomb were covered in strange alien hieroglyphs—twisted, angular symbols that seemed to shift and wriggle when viewed from different angles. As Davros gazed at them, the whispers began again. This time, it was as if the walls themselves were calling to him, the words almost familiar, like a language he once knew but could no longer remember.

"They're... alive," Davros murmured, a chill creeping up his spine.

"What's that, Major?" asked Sergeant Tyne, one of his most reliable men, his voice trembling as he turned to look at Davros.

"The tomb," Davros replied, his voice barely above a whisper. "It's... alive."

The team pushed forward, deeper into the tomb, as the atmosphere grew heavier, the shadows darker. The flickering light of their torches cast eerie reflections on the walls, distorting the symbols into grotesque, ever-shifting shapes. The farther they went, the more the whispers intensified, until they were all speaking in unison, an alien chorus reverberating in Davros's skull.

Then, the ground beneath them rumbled, and the walls trembled.

A figure appeared from the shadows—a mechanical guardian, its body a twisted amalgamation of metal and bone. Its face was a hollow mask, empty sockets glowing with an unearthly green light. The Necron Deathmark had awoken.

Before Davros or anyone could react, the creature moved with unnatural speed, its body flashing forward and slamming into one of the soldiers. Tyne, who had been leading the formation, was caught off guard. The Deathmark's elongated, razor-sharp limbs sliced through his armor like paper, and in the blink of an eye, Tyne's body was split in half, blood and metal raining down as the screams of his comrades echoed through the tomb.

The rest of the squad opened fire, but the Necron guardian was too fast, its movements too erratic and precise. The air was filled with the sound of bolter fire, explosions, and the unholy screech of the Deathmark as it tore into the team, dismembering them with terrifying efficiency.

Davros staggered back, his heart pounding as the last of his men fell. There was nothing they could do. This... this was beyond them.

With a roar, Davros charged forward, his bolter roaring to life as he unloaded rounds into the creature's chest. The shots did little more than spark off its armored exterior. His mind screamed for an answer, but none came.

As the last scream of his fallen comrade echoed through the chamber, the tomb's gates slammed shut with an awful finality, sealing them inside.

The moment the gates slammed shut, sealing Davros and his remaining squad inside the tomb, a palpable weight fell over the team. The once-murderous whispers grew louder, swirling around them like a heavy fog. The walls, cold and unyielding, seemed to hum with a low, guttural vibration, resonating deep in Davros's bones. His bolter hung loosely in his grip, his fingers trembling, but not from fear. There was something else—a strange connection, like his mind was being pulled into the walls themselves. The artefact in his pack pulsed again, its sickly green glow lighting up the corridor in waves, as if it were a beacon summoning something ancient.

"Major, we need to move!" Sergeant Kael's voice sliced through the tension. He was the last of his men still standing, his armor battered, but intact. Sweat beaded on his forehead as his eyes darted nervously around the shifting corridors.

Davros didn't respond immediately. His eyes were locked on the walls—those same alien glyphs that were now glowing faintly, twisting as if alive. They seemed to watch him, the symbols stretching, distorting in unnatural ways. And behind those symbols, he could almost hear the low hum of machinery—an ancient, alien mechanism slowly awakening.

"Major!" Kael barked again, snapping Davros back to the present. He shook his head, his vision momentarily flickering with darkness.

"We move," Davros said, his voice low, almost inaudible. But as he turned, he could feel the cold crawl of something unnatural through his veins. It was as though the very air in the tomb was alive, suffocating him. His body, already augmented with cybernetics, began to ache, each joint grinding and protesting in ways it never had before.

They moved forward, bolters raised, but as they did, the corridors seemed to stretch and shift before them. What had once been a linear path now twisted like a maze, the walls distorting, growing longer and narrower. Each turn led them deeper into the heart of the tomb, and the sense of isolation grew heavier. The air felt thick with the power of something ancient—something alive— and Davros felt the weight of it pressing in on his mind.

Suddenly, without warning, mechanical claws shot out from the walls. They were fast, sharp—too fast. The first to fall was Corporal Hadrian, who was ripped from the front of the formation.

His scream was cut short as the claws tore through his body, dragging him into the darkness. His blood sprayed across the stone, the walls absorbing it with a sickening slowness. Kael fired, but his shots went wide. The claws retreated as quickly as they came, vanishing back into the shadows. Hadrian was gone.

"Move!" Davros shouted, his voice raw with urgency.

But as they sprinted down the corridor, the walls shifted again. The tomb seemed to bend, twisting the very nature of reality around them. They stumbled through the now-elongated hallways, their steps growing erratic, as if the tomb itself were alive, aware of their every move. The voices—those low, vibrating whispers—grew louder, until they were deafening, and it was no longer clear if the words were coming from the tomb or from his own mind.

Then, another claw burst from the floor beneath them, this time catching Corporal Gage by the leg. He screamed, his voice broken by the sharp metal that impaled him, pinning him to the ground. Kael and Davros fired desperately, but it was too late. The claw twisted, and Gage was torn in half, his blood spraying across the walls.

Davros's stomach churned, but the horror felt distant, as if it were happening to someone else. His vision blurred, the edges of his sight growing dark and hazy. He blinked hard, trying to focus, but the tomb was warping around him, bending in ways it shouldn't. The walls stretched, pulling inward like the maw of a hungry beast, closing in on them.

Then, a shuddering, metallic voice rumbled through the air, vibrating through the stone like a distant thunderstorm. It was an ancient voice, one Davros knew instinctively, even if he had never heard it before.

"You belong to us now."

The words echoed in his skull, rattling his thoughts. His fingers twitched, involuntarily gripping his bolter tighter. A sudden, sharp pain shot through his spine, a searing jolt that made him stagger.

"Get your head in the game, Major!" Kael shouted, but the panic in his voice was unmistakable. His eyes were wild, searching the shadows for any sign of movement.

The pain in Davros's body intensified, crawling through the cybernetic implants, like something inside him was being triggered—something *alien*. His augmented muscles twitched and spasmed as the eerie whispers filled his ears again, now loud enough to drown out the sounds of his men's frantic footsteps. It wasn't just the tomb's power. It was something inside him—a call. The artefact. The Necron technology buried in his body, responding to the tomb's power.

Davros's breath hitched. He could feel it now—the artefact wasn't just a tool. It was a key. A key to the tomb's horrors. He could feel the strange connection between his body and the walls, as though he was no longer fully human, no longer fully alive.

Kael turned back to look at him, his face pale beneath his helmet. "Major, what's happening to you?"

Davros opened his mouth to speak, but the words caught in his throat. He wanted to scream, to tell Kael to run, but instead, his mouth betrayed him. His voice came out as a distorted rasp, a mix of his own voice and something ancient, something cold.

"*I am... becoming part of it.*"

And with that, the tomb's shifting walls closed in tighter around them, the metallic voice echoing through every inch of space.

The heavy doors to the Rubicon Spire's med-lab hissed open, and Davros stumbled through, clutching the artefact like a lifeline. His body was a warzone, every muscle and nerve burned with alien energy, the Necron tech coursing through him in a way that felt both intoxicating and horrifying. His squad was gone. Kael, Gage, the others—all dead. Torn apart by the tomb's deadly traps, or consumed by the mechanical monstrosities lurking in the shadows. Their screams still echoed in his mind, their deaths his fault. He had led them here, and now he was the only one left. Alone.

As he staggered through the halls, the whispers of the Warp mingled with the cold, methodical hum of the Necron technology inside him. It was maddening. At times, the voices were a single entity, shrieking from the depths of the immaterium. At other moments, they were fractured, a cacophony of demands, promises, and threats. But always, they clawed at his sanity, never letting him rest.

He tried to block it out, focusing instead on the mission. He needed to return the artefact. That was all that mattered now. The voices would stop once he fulfilled his purpose. Wouldn't they?

The deeper he moved into the Spire, the more he realized something was wrong. The usual sterile coldness of the station felt warped, somehow. The walls shifted and pulsated beneath his fingers. He could feel the Spire itself... watching him. Responding to him. His augmented body was no longer his own. It moved as though guided by unseen hands, his arms and legs twitching, jerking at odd angles. The more the Necron artefact's influence grew, the more his humanity slipped away.

Finally, he arrived at Dr. Celeste Thorn's private lab, the cold steel doors silently parting as he approached. She was waiting for him inside, standing with her back to him, staring at a data pad. Her white lab coat swayed slightly in the breeze generated by the air vents. She didn't look up as Davros entered.

"You're late," she said in her usual, calculated tone. "Did you enjoy your little trip to the tomb, Major?"

Davros's heart skipped a beat. He didn't respond immediately, his mind scrambling to understand the growing sense of betrayal gnawing at him. The pieces were starting to fall into place—his team had been sent to die. The artefact wasn't a relic. It was a weapon. And he was the target.

Uno Nguyen © 2024

"You knew," Davros rasped, his voice filled with growing disgust. His hand tightened around the artefact in his pack, the green glow still pulsing, still *calling* to him. "You knew what this was all along. You knew what it would do to us."

Dr. Thorn finally turned to face him, her eyes glittering with something that could almost be mistaken for amusement. She crossed the room toward him with slow, deliberate steps. "You think this was about your *team*, Major?" Her voice was like silk, but her words cut like steel. "No, this was always about you. You were chosen. You were meant to become more than you were."

Davros staggered back, the weight of her words sinking in like a blade lodged in his gut. He wanted to scream, to lash out, but his augmented body felt... wrong. His chest burned as if something inside him were *growing*, pulsing with alien rhythm, sending shivers through his spine. The Necron tech was spreading through him, taking root in his very bones.

"Your body," Thorn continued, her gaze cold and unblinking, "was never meant to be human, Davros. The Rubicon procedure is just the beginning. The artefact you brought back will complete the transformation. The Necron technology inside you is awakening, as it was always meant to. You can either accept it, embrace it... or die as a failed experiment."

Her words twisted through his mind, mixing with the whispers from the Warp, the voices rising and falling in violent harmonies. He could feel his flesh and bones *shift*, the machinery within him responding to her command. He was becoming something else. Something monstrous.

"No... this isn't me. I am... Davros Phaedrus, Deathwatch," he whispered, his voice trembling as he tried to fight the invasion of his body and mind.

Thorn's lips curled into a thin smile. "Davros Phaedrus is dead. What you are now is far greater. You *will* transcend, just like the others. Don't you understand? The Rubicon was never about saving you. It was about pushing the limits. And you're just the first."

Davros's vision flickered, the room warping as his body spasmed, the sheer weight of the transformations overwhelming him. His heart raced, but it was no longer under his control. His legs buckled, forcing him to one knee as his arm shot out, his fingers twitching like they had a mind of their own. The Necron tech inside him fought for dominance, and his flesh began to merge with the mechanical augmentations. His heart screamed for release, but it was trapped in a prison of flesh and wire.

"You were never meant to survive this," Thorn's voice echoed cruelly through the growing madness in his mind.

Davros's mind cracked open like a ripe fruit, his soul torn between the voices of the Warp, the cold logic of the Necrons, and his own desperate attempts to cling to some shred of humanity. He reached for his bolter, but his hand faltered, trembling.

Thorn stepped closer, her gaze unblinking. "You *are* mine now, Major. You belong to the Rubicon Corporation."

As she reached out to touch the side of his face, his body jerked away. He felt something inside him snap—*something* inside him was gone, and he was no longer sure whether it was his sanity or his soul.

"You can't make me..." Davros whispered through clenched teeth.

Thorn smiled, almost lovingly. "You already belong to something far greater, Davros. You're no longer human. You're *evolution.*"

The dark whispers grew louder again, and the shadows in the corners of the room seemed to stir, reaching for him. They were calling to him now. The Necron tech. The Warp. His own fractured mind. All of it was pulling him under, a suffocating tide.

Davros's mind was a cacophony of chaos. The room around him seemed to *melt*, the walls undulating like they were alive. He could feel his augmented body tremble under the pressure, each nerve firing in jagged, painful bursts. The warp-saturated artefact pulsed in his pack, its sickly green light throbbing like a heartbeat, syncing with the thrumming madness inside him.

He couldn't stand it anymore. The whispers. The *flesh* growing inside him. The unbearable weight of the Necron tech, the relentless push of the Warp, gnawing away at his humanity.

"I need to destroy it," Davros muttered under his breath, his voice barely audible over the howls in his head. His hands were slick with sweat, fingers trembling as they gripped the bolter strapped to his waist. He had to get rid of the artefact. It was the only way.

His steps were unsteady as he moved toward the containment chamber, the room's cold sterile lights flickering overhead. The once familiar hallways of the Spire now seemed foreign to him, warped and twisted by the lingering influence of the Necron device. The air around him felt thick, like it was pressing in on him, suffocating him. And yet, he pressed on, determined to sever the link between himself and the cursed artefact.

As he reached the lab's center, his fingers fumbled at the straps of his pack, pulling the artefact free. It *burned* in his hands— its surface scorching to the touch, like holding a piece of the sun itself. But Davros didn't care. He needed to destroy it.

With a growl of frustration, he threw the artefact to the ground, stomping on it with all his might. The moment his boot made contact, a violent surge of energy erupted from the device, a wave of power that sent him crashing backwards into the wall. The room pulsed with sickly green light, and the air filled with an unnatural hum as the Warp, too, reacted to his defiance.

The artefact trembled, its form warping and distorting as the energies it contained clawed free from their prison. The reality around him flickered like an old vid-screen, and then—*suddenly*—he was no longer in the lab.

Uno Nguyen © 2024

He was somewhere else. Somewhere *wrong*.

A barren landscape stretched out before him, its horizon jagged and broken like the remnants of a shattered world. The ground was cracked and bleeding, as if the very earth had been torn apart by some unseen hand. In the distance, he saw the flicker of movement—vast, hulking shapes stumbling forward on mechanical limbs. As they grew closer, Davros saw them for what they were: *cybernetic horrors*, grotesque and fused with twisted machines. Their bodies were mismatched, limbs of flesh and steel, faces frozen in eternal, twisted screams.

He felt a shudder of recognition deep within him. They were *him*—his future. The mutation, the transformation that had already begun within him, now fully realized.

A voice—cold and mocking—echoed through the desolate landscape. It was a voice that seemed to come from all around him, warping and shifting like the sound of a thousand voices in the Warp.

"You've done well, *Davros*," it sneered, the name twisting into something unholy. "Look at what you've become. This is your destiny."

Davros's mind reeled. This wasn't real. It couldn't be real. But as the figures in the distance drew closer, their faces became clearer—twisted reflections of his own, each one grinning as if they had already won. His pulse quickened, his vision blurred, and his body burned. The machine inside him *called*—it wanted this. It wanted him to join them. To lead them.

Another voice—this one darker, more powerful—spoke in his mind. It was a voice he had heard before, though he could never quite place it.

"You can lead them, Davros. You can control this. You were always meant to. All this power. All this *might*. All for you."

Davros clenched his fists, his body trembling, the wires and metal beneath his skin aching as the transformation surged again. His breath quickened, and his fingers twitched toward the bolter still strapped to his waist. *No*—he had to resist. This was a trap. The Necron, the Warp—it was all part of the same twisted game. A game that he had no intention of playing.

But before he could act, the figures before him stopped. They were silent now. Watching. And then one stepped forward. A grotesque, monstrous version of himself, its face half-metal, half-flesh, the features warped and barely recognizable. Its eyes gleamed with the same green light as the artefact.

"You were always meant to lead," it whispered, its voice a dark mockery of his own. "You cannot escape this. This is your *offering.*"

As it spoke, the ground beneath Davros's feet cracked open, revealing the maw of an ancient, glimmering device—a Necron tomb, pulsing with dark energies. He could feel the pull of it, the irresistible gravity dragging him closer, tugging at his very soul.

"No," he gasped, staggering back. "I—*I am not you.*"

The creature, the twisted version of himself, let out a guttural laugh, its mouth stretching impossibly wide.

"You are already mine," it hissed, its voice like the sound of grinding metal. "*You were always meant to lead.*"

And as the vision closed around him, the light from the artefact surged once more, blinding him, suffocating him, until all that remained was a whispering darkness.

The Rubicon Spire was a dying thing. Its heart was a ruptured organ, gushing Warp energy, bleeding madness into every crevice. The air was thick with a viscous fog, and the walls—once sterile and gleaming with cold, clinical efficiency—now groaned under the weight of reality itself, bending and warping as if in excruciating pain. Red emergency lights flickered in rhythm with the pulsing thrum of the artefact, now embedded deep within Davros's chest, its presence a constant ache, a gnawing hunger in his very bones.

The chaos was beyond anything he had ever witnessed. The Spire was collapsing around him—screams echoed through the hallways, punctuated by the sharp crack of gunfire and the sickening *splat* of flesh and metal. Necron warriors, once entombed in their ancient crypts, were awakening, their skeletal bodies encased in living metal. They marched forward with a terrifying precision, their weapons crackling with deadly energy, their eyes glowing with malevolent green fire.

Amidst them, the air shuddered as if reality itself was beginning to tear. Through the breach, the Warp spilled forth—a horrific tide of Chaos, twisting and distorting the very fabric of space. Monstrous, formless creatures of dark power oozed from the rift, their limbs writhing like serpents, mouths opening and closing with gurgled laughter, their voices a chorus of madness.

Davros stood alone in the center of it all. His once-human body, now grotesquely altered, was a patchwork of flesh, metal, and dark energy. His left arm was a mass of hydraulic limbs and circuits, twitching with every motion. His face, or what remained of it, was a cracked mask of human features, distorted and bloodied, the skin stretched unnaturally taut as if it no longer belonged to him. His eyes, once dull and controlled, now burned with the eerie green glow of the artefact, like twin stars of unnatural energy.

But there was no time to reflect on what he had become. The Spire was crumbling. The screams of his fellow survivors rang out, and in the distance, the twisted figures of his once-allies, now fully corrupted and mutated by the Warp, clashed with Necron soldiers. The final battle was unfolding, and he was at the heart of it, the artefact pulsing in his chest like a living bomb, ready to explode.

"I am the weapon now." The thought came to him with cold clarity, his body a vessel of destruction, an instrument of death that had long since ceased to be a man. His fingers twitched, and he

realized his hand was reaching for the trigger—a trigger buried deep within his own skin, within the very core of the artefact. But there was a choice, a final moment of control.

Destroy it... or unleash it?

The Necron forces advanced, their relentless march unceasing. In the shadows, Davros could see the flickers of Chaos warbands charging toward the heart of the Spire. The Warp crackled violently, and a piercing howl split the air as one of the great Chaos creatures, a hulking beast of sinew and corrupted flesh, tore its way through the walls, its maw dripping with the blood of its victims.

It was all collapsing. The walls, the systems, his sanity—everything was coming undone.

Davros's chest burned. His body screamed as the Warp tore at the remaining threads of his consciousness. The artefact, now almost fused to his soul, was a maelstrom of power, a weapon capable of obliterating everything around him. *Too much power, too much temptation.* He felt the Chaos Gods whispering in his mind, offering him dominion, offering him victory over the ruins of the Spire. He could feel their fingers gripping at him, offering him a place at their side, eternal power. *He could lead them all.*

But Davros knew better.

He *knew* what this was. It was not power. It was *corruption.* It was the end of everything he had ever sworn to protect, everything he had ever *been.* If he let this consume him, if he let the Warp take full control, the galaxy would be no better than a carcass, picked apart by Chaos and the Necron.

The only way to end it was to destroy the artefact. To sacrifice himself before the insanity of it consumed everything. He would not be the harbinger of the end—he would end it himself.

But it was too late.

A *screech* erupted from the depths of the Spire. The artefact flared, its green light blinding, then pulsed violently, thrumming in sync with the beat of his heart. His fingers were no longer in control, his body no longer his own. The power of the device surged up his spine, fusing with his mind, ripping apart his humanity, warping him into something *other*.

He heard voices again—voices from the dark, the hollow whisperings of the Necron Overlords, the mocking laughter of the Chaos Gods. The energies inside him were too much. The Warp's forces had already seeped into his soul.

He had become the instrument of the apocalypse.

With one final, futile push, Davros activated the core of the artefact. The ground shook. The ceiling above him shattered, and a torrent of fire and blood erupted, consuming everything in its path. The air itself screamed as the warpstorm exploded outward in a massive, world-rending detonation.

The Spire—the place that had become his prison, his tomb— was obliterated, its shattered remains falling like ash through the void of space. The explosion was a final cry of agony, a storm of destruction that tore apart the very fabric of the Spire and anything in its wake.

In the aftermath, the station was a graveyard. Nothing remained but the flickering remains of the Spire's shattered hull, drifting like a broken husk in the cold expanse of space.

Amid the ruins, one figure remained—an empty husk of flesh and metal, broken and burned.

As the last remnants of the explosion's flames faded into the void, the final thought echoed through Davros's fractured mind. It wasn't a prayer. It wasn't a plea for redemption.

It was a truth he had always known.

"I've become everything I swore to destroy."

Uno Nguyen © 2024

THE CRAWLING DARK

Davros awoke with a start. His first breath was ragged, a sharp inhale that burned his lungs. For a moment, he thought he was still dreaming, lost in the suffocating haze of the Warp. But when his vision cleared, reality bled through in waves of sickening clarity.

He lay in a barren, windswept wasteland, the sky above choked with ash and smoldering remnants of the Rubicon Spire. The once-glorious station that had been his prison was now a shattered carcass, its skeletal remains drifting across the heavens like some forgotten monument to mankind's hubris. The Spire's death throes had ripped open the fabric of space, but the destruction had not been kind to him. His body... it felt wrong. Worse than before. He could feel the alien whispers inside him, echoes of the Necron Overlords who had begun to speak through his very flesh.

His mind was a fragmented mess, memories slipping through his fingers like sand. His body, though augmented beyond recognition, was now something more than human. Flesh and metal twisted together in grotesque harmony, the artifact embedded within his chest now a part of him, an agonizing presence that gnawed at his very soul.

The pain was unrelenting, but it was the whispers—cold, alien voices that spoke in the back of his mind—that terrified him the most. Their words were distant at first, like the rustle of dead leaves in the wind, but they grew louder, more insistent.

"You are ours... You will serve us, Davros Phaedrus... All that you were has died. Your body is our vessel. Your will, our weapon..."

He gritted his teeth, trying to push them out, but they only grew stronger. The voices of the Necron Overlords, their ancient minds reaching through the Warp, using his own body as a conduit.

"Come to us, warrior. The tomb calls to you. The machines are awake. Join us..."

Davros squeezed his eyes shut, forcing himself to ignore the voices, but it was as if they were etched into his very mind. They were part of him now, forever tied to the horrors of the Necron, to the Warp's corrupting touch. He could no longer escape them.

The landscape around him was no better than the hell inside his mind. Jagged spires of blackened metal jutted from the ground, remnants of a long-dead civilization. The ruins stretched out for miles, a world now desolate, its once-vibrant soul ripped away by the encroaching darkness. Crimson clouds churned above, casting a hellish glow over everything. The air was thick with the scent of burnt ozone and decay.

He pushed himself to his feet, his limbs stiff and alien, the weight of his cybernetic enhancements dragging him down. The faint hum of power radiated from his body, and a surge of agony rippled through him as the Necron technology embedded deep within his bones responded to some unseen command. His hands twitched, fingers aching, but they moved. They always moved now, as if they belonged to something greater than himself.

"Where are they?" Davros muttered under his breath.

His heart pounded in his chest, the twisted metal that now formed part of his ribcage creaking with every movement. The Rubicon Corporation would have followed him. They couldn't let the artefact go, not after everything they had done to him. They would send someone to reclaim it, to claim him.

And then, through the fog of his shattered mind, he heard them.

Footsteps.

The dull, rhythmic thud of boots on the cracked earth. His body tensed, the metallic arm itching for a weapon, any weapon. He reached for his bolter, but it was gone, lost in the inferno when the Spire had exploded. He was weaponless, trapped in the dark, his own body now an enemy.

The soldiers that emerged from the shadows were not the men he remembered. They were twisted, hunched figures, their bodies an amalgamation of cybernetics and flesh. The Rubicon soldiers—corrupted, mutated, their bodies no longer human, but something far worse. Their features were gaunt, eyes hollow, and their mouths were stretched into twisted, mechanical grins. The corruption had taken hold, their augments twitching and spasming unnaturally, and the Warp's taint hung around them like a stench, a dark aura that suffocated the air.

"Davros…" one of them croaked, his voice weak, unrecognizable. The soldier staggered forward, his body jerking violently with every step. His cybernetic limbs were misshapen, one of his arms stretched unnaturally long, the other crushed under the weight of the metal augments that had overtaken his body. "Please… don't—don't leave us. We… We… I can't…"

Davros's eyes narrowed as he looked at the soldier. He saw the flicker of recognition in the man's eyes—an old face, a fleeting memory of comrades he had once fought beside. But now… this was no soldier. This was a monster, a hollow shell of what had once been human.

The soldier's face contorted in agony as his chest suddenly expanded, the sound of wiring and bone snapping loudly as it split open. Black ichor spilled from his mouth, a grotesque mass of wires and synthetic flesh erupted from his body, and then, with a final, deafening scream, the soldier's entire form detonated in a shower of mechanical limbs, corrupted flesh, and foul liquid.

Davros didn't flinch.

He couldn't. There was nothing left of the man, just a twisted heap of wreckage. And in the moment before the explosion, before the soldier's final words fell silent, Davros heard something—a whisper, soft and chilling—cut through the shriek of agony.

"No mercy... left here."

Davros turned away from the burning remains, the acrid smoke filling his lungs. He didn't mourn the man's death. He couldn't afford to. There was no mercy left for any of them, not for him, not for anyone in this ruined world.

He continued his march through the wasteland, his twisted form moving with purpose. The Rubicon soldiers, the corrupted remnants of his former comrades, would keep coming for him. The Necron voices would keep calling to him. And the Warp, always whispering, always coaxing, would never stop.

The dark was crawling toward him, and there was nowhere left to hide.

The Imperial Guard outpost was silent. Too silent.

Davros stepped over the threshold, the iron door creaking on its hinges, the air thick with the smell of old blood and rust. The scent of decay clung to the walls like a permanent stain, a lingering reminder of the horror that had unfolded here. It was clear the station had once been a hub of activity, but now it was a tomb—its former inhabitants now little more than twisted statues, their forms frozen in the throes of a death they hadn't seen coming.

Uno Nguyen © 2024

The walls were adorned with faded banners, now torn and hanging limply, their once-vibrant colors dulled by soot and time. The place had been hastily abandoned, but the damage was far from accidental. The remnants of men and women—guardsmen—lay scattered across the room, their bodies grotesquely altered. Some were still in their armor, but their bones and flesh had been fused with the machinery they once wore, welded together by some unknown, unholy force.

Davros's gaze lingered on the bodies—one man's hand, stretched unnaturally long, had become part of his lasgun, the weapon now a grotesque extension of his body. Another soldier's face was half-hidden beneath a mask of metal, the skin stretched tight across the contours of his skull, the eyes hollow and staring as if still waiting for the next order.

The horror was overwhelming, but it wasn't just the mutilations that made Davros uneasy. It was the silence. The sense that something was watching him. Something ancient. The Necrons.

He moved cautiously, his boots crunching over the broken remnants of fallen equipment. A strange buzzing hum filled the air, distant but palpable, like the reverberations of an alien machine waking up. He had felt it before—after the destruction of the Rubicon Spire—when the artifact had first begun to change him. The Necrons were stirring.

A noise echoed in the far corner of the room. A voice. Weak. And yet it carried with it an unmistakable sense of urgency.

"Help... help me..." The voice was trembling, broken, like a man clinging to the last fragments of sanity.

Davros turned toward the sound, stepping carefully through the wreckage. In the far corner of the outpost, a single man sat hunched over, his body slumped in a corner, staring at the bloodstained floor. His uniform was torn, his face gaunt, eyes wide with madness. A guardsman, the last of them, perhaps.

Uno Nguyen © 2024

As Davros approached, the man looked up, his eyes darting nervously, as though he couldn't decide whether to speak or run. His lips trembled.

"You... you're not one of them, are you?" the guardsman rasped, his voice a ragged whisper. "You're... you're still... human..."

Davros said nothing, but his eyes scanned the man's disfigured form. The guardsman's face was half-hidden beneath a mask of mechanical implants, and his arms had been twisted into jagged, metallic appendages, the wiring and tubes that ran through his veins humming softly.

"They came... they came from beneath the ground," the man continued, his voice growing more frantic. "They were sleeping... until the signal. Then they awoke. The Necrons... they're terraforming the planet... turning it into a Tomb World. This place... this place is just the beginning. You can't stop it."

Davros took a step closer. "The Necrons?" he murmured, as if tasting the name for the first time, like it was a curse. He had heard the stories, the ancient legends, but hearing them here—hearing them from someone who had witnessed their awakening—felt different.

The guardsman's breathing grew erratic, his hands shaking as he reached out, his fingers twitching, as though he were trying to grasp onto something that wasn't there. His eyes widened, staring at something only he could see.

"They know... they know you're here..." he muttered, his words barely coherent. "You're the harbinger... The... the one who brings death. You... you..."

Before Davros could respond, the man's body spasmed violently. His chest bulged as if something were pushing its way out from inside him. Metal tendrils, slick with oil and blood, erupted from his torso, wrapping around his limbs, pulling him into the shadows. The man's scream was choked off as his body was yanked

Uno Nguyen © 2024

into the darkness, the tendrils dragging him away with unholy strength.

Davros was left standing in the dimly lit room, his heart pounding. He could hear the scraping of metal against stone, the echoing sound of the mechanical tendrils pulling the man's body deeper into the walls, as though the very structure of the outpost had been infected by the same malevolent force.

For a long moment, Davros remained still, his mind racing. He knew now, without a doubt, that the Necrons had returned. And they had not just awakened—they were reshaping this world into something that no longer resembled humanity.

The rhythmic hum of distant Monoliths filled the air now, growing louder with each passing second. The noise was almost hypnotic, like a heartbeat coming from the depths of the planet itself, as if the world were alive with the waking of ancient machines. The ground beneath Davros's feet trembled ever so slightly, and his breath caught in his throat. His cybernetic enhancements screamed at him, a primal warning that pulsed through his veins.

"They're coming," he whispered, his voice trembling with the weight of the knowledge he now carried. The Necrons were not just awakening—they were *calling* to him. Drawing him deeper into their web.

And he had no choice but to answer.

The landscape was barren, a twisted mirror of a world that had once been alive with hope. Jagged rocks jutted from the ground like broken teeth, and the skies above, heavy with swirling clouds, were stained a sickly green—a sign of something ancient and foul awakening beneath the surface. The distant rumble of Necron Monoliths reverberated through the earth, a sound that seemed to crawl beneath the skin and into the very marrow of Davros's bones.

The voices were getting louder.

Uno Nguyen © 2024

Whispers, soft at first, like the rustling of dry leaves, grew in volume and urgency with every step he took. His augmented body—a blend of flesh and machine, already distorted beyond recognition—seemed to react to the very ground he walked on. His limbs ached, his mind fractured with flashes of visions he couldn't fully comprehend. The Chaos Gods were speaking to him, each one vying for his attention, each one offering him something different, something tempting.

Khorne's voice was a thunderous roar, filled with the clang of steel and the pounding of drums. *"Blood, Davros. Blood for the Blood God! All who stand in your path shall be shattered like bone beneath your boot. Power beyond your wildest dreams awaits, if you but submit."*

Davros clenched his fists, his metal fingers digging into his flesh, but he pressed on, ignoring the lure of violence, the hunger for destruction that surged in his chest.

Then came **Slaanesh**, soft and silken, like the caress of velvet against his skin. *"Freedom from pain, Davros. Cast aside the agony that clings to you. Pleasure, unending. I can give you release. I can give you eternity, free from the weight of your broken flesh."*

The very thought of surrendering to such excess made him shudder. It was a false promise—one that would twist him further, turn him into nothing more than a slave to indulgence.

Nurgle was next, his voice heavy and wet, dripping with the sweetness of rot. *"Peace, Davros. The suffering of this world is fleeting, but under my guidance, you will find eternal peace. No more pain. No more fear. Let go of your resistance. Accept my embrace."*

Davros's skin crawled at the thought of Nurgle's gift—corruption, decay, and eternal stagnation. It was the antithesis of everything he had fought for. And yet, a part of him could feel the temptation—how easy it would be to let go and sink into the eternal sleep of oblivion.

Finally, **Tzeentch's** voice, sharp and deceptive, slithered into his mind. "*Control, Davros. I can give you control over your fate. You are not a pawn. You are the master of your destiny. With my knowledge, you can rewrite the stars themselves.*"

But Davros was not so easily swayed. He had tasted the power of the Warp, and he knew its promises were lies, wrapped in gold and destruction. He rejected them all. With a final mental cry of defiance, he pushed them out of his mind. Their voices fell silent, but the weight of their whispers lingered like a shadow in the back of his mind, gnawing at his resolve.

He could not afford to be distracted now. The Monoliths loomed ahead, their towering forms casting long, jagged shadows over the ruined landscape. He had come to this forsaken place with a single purpose: to confront the Necrons and end their curse. Whether it was for vengeance, or something deeper—something tied to his very existence—he couldn't say. But the path before him was clear.

The ground trembled beneath his feet as he reached the foot of the largest Monolith. The massive, pyramid-like structure hummed with power, its surface covered in ancient, cryptic symbols that seemed to pulse with a life of their own. At the apex of the Monolith, an eerie green light flickered, and Davros felt his heart race, not with fear, but with a cold anticipation.

From within the depths of the Monolith, a voice boomed— mechanical, but somehow filled with an ancient, unyielding presence. It spoke his name.

"*Davros Phaedrus.*" The voice echoed through the valley, reverberating off the jagged rocks around him. "*You are an imperfect vessel. A creation of corrupted flesh. What you seek is beyond you. You are nothing but a tool—a tool that will complete its purpose, as all things do.*"

The voice seemed to come from everywhere at once, filling his head, his chest, his very soul. Davros's mind reeled, but he steeled himself, refusing to bend.

"I am not your tool," he growled, though his voice was shaky. The words felt foreign, even to him. Was this what he had become? A tool for something greater, something far beyond his control?

Suddenly, the ground cracked open beneath him, and from the chasm rose Necron constructs—metallic horrors, their skeletal frames glistening with unnatural light. Their cold, dead eyes focused on Davros as they advanced, their arms raised in unison, their weapons crackling with energy.

A massive Necron Overlord stepped forward, its golden mask gleaming in the greenish glow of the Monolith. Its voice reverberated through the air, deep and foreboding.

"We are the Necron, Davros Phaedrus. And you will be one of us. Your flesh will be remade, your mind reprogrammed. We will complete you."

Davros's heart hammered in his chest, and for a moment, doubt seeped into his mind. The Overlord's words were cold, final. But Davros refused to fall prey to despair. He would fight. Even if his flesh and soul were torn apart, he would resist.

The Necron constructs closed in, and in that moment, the true horror of their mission became clear. They weren't merely here to kill him—they were here to reshape him, to turn him into one of them.

Pain erupted as cold metal claws ripped into his body, cutting through the skin, severing muscle, tearing at his bones. The agony was unimaginable, a perfect fusion of flesh and metal. His mind screamed in protest as the Necron machines began their cruel modifications, grafting pieces of cold, alien technology into his body. But as the Overlord watched, its expression unreadable, Davros's resolve hardened.

They could break his body, he thought, *but they could never break his will.*

Uno Nguyen © 2024

Through the pain and the chaos, he let out a roar—a defiant, guttural sound that reverberated through the tomb. He would not be their tool. He would *never* be their puppet.

"I am not your tool!" he shouted again, his voice echoing with the fury of his defiance. It was a cry of rebellion, a refusal to bend to the whims of the Necron Overlord or any god, Chaos or otherwise.

Davros staggered through the barren landscape, his body trembling, blood seeping from fresh wounds where Necron constructs had torn into him. His chest heaved, his augmented heart beating erratically as the world around him seemed to twist and contort. The greenish hue of the sky was fading, consumed by an unnatural darkness.

He had escaped—barely. But what was escape if there was nowhere to run? His mind was unraveling, gnawed at by the ceaseless whispers of the Warp, by the grinding hunger of the Necrons, by the suffocating weight of his own existence. He could feel their presence behind him, the cold metallic eyes of the Necrons, the oppressive gaze of the Chaos Gods, always watching, always whispering.

He stumbled forward, too weak to fight, too broken to resist. The landscape shifted as he moved, the very ground beneath him warping and folding. He couldn't tell where the horizon ended and the earth began. His vision blurred, and when he blinked, the world changed, shifting like a reflection in broken glass.

Then he saw it.

The forest was not a forest at all, but a twisting distortion of the Warp itself. Towering trees of blackened, gnarled roots rose like jagged spires, their trunks slick with a dark, viscous substance that pulsed in time with his erratic heartbeat. The air was thick with whispers, voices that seemed to bleed from the very soil beneath him, too many to count. The ground squelched beneath his boots, as if alive—alive and waiting.

Uno Nguyen © 2024

As he took his first step into the forest, a chill ran down his spine. The trees bent toward him, their shadows stretching unnaturally long. His mind swam with flashes of memories—some real, some not—of lives he had lived, of battles he had fought, of deaths he had caused. Each vision was like a shard of glass, cutting into his mind, distorting his sense of self.

A shadow loomed ahead, stretching and twisting, as if it were a living thing. Then the whisper came, soft at first, but growing louder with each passing second.

"Davros..."

He froze. His heart stopped.

It was his voice. But it wasn't his voice.

From the darkness emerged a figure, its form an abomination of flesh and metal, twisted beyond recognition. It moved with unnatural grace, the Warp dripping from its every movement. The face—if it could be called that—was his. Or at least, it once had been. But the features were distorted, corrupted by the insidious touch of the Warp. His eyes were black, voids of nothingness, and his mouth stretched into a cruel grin.

"You should have known, Davros," the figure whispered, its voice a mocking echo of his own. **"You were never meant to escape. This, all of this, is your fate. The cycle is endless. The chains are already forged. You are only a moment in eternity."**

Davros staggered back, unable to tear his eyes away from the monstrosity. His own form. His own face. But what had it become? What had he become?

The figure stepped closer, and with each step, the world around them warped further, the trees groaning and shifting like creatures in pain. The roots of the forest recoiled at its presence. **"You think you can escape? You think you can change anything?"** It raised its arms, and the forest seemed to react, the shadows clawing at the air. **"You've seen what's to come. Your**

Uno Nguyen © 2024

power, your flesh, your very soul—corrupted. You'll lead the universe into ruin, or you'll be its downfall. Either way, you are nothing but a cog in a machine that cannot be stopped."

Davros gritted his teeth, refusing to let the creature—this abomination—have any sway over him. He raised his arm, feeling the pulsing energy of the Warp coursing through him, but it felt... alien. Foreign. Like it wasn't his to command anymore.

"**No.**" His voice was hoarse, but defiant. "I am not you. I'm *nothing like you*."

The figure laughed, a chilling, hollow sound. "**Oh, but you are. You always have been.**"

As the figure spoke, the world around Davros began to crack. The trees around him split open, revealing shattered glimpses of alternate realities—futures that seemed to shimmer and distort like broken mirrors.

In one vision, Davros saw himself as a monstrous warlord, draped in dark armor, leading an army of twisted machines across a burning galaxy. His eyes burned with the fire of madness, and the screams of the dying echoed in his ears.

In another, he saw the galaxy consumed by Chaos. Worlds turned to ash, civilizations broken, and in the center of it all, the Warp storm howled, devouring everything in its path. And in that storm, Davros stood as a ruler, surrounded by the twisted faces of the dead.

But there was one more vision. A quiet one, almost peaceful in its sorrow. Humanity, wiped from existence entirely, the stars silent in their eternal cold. There was no war, no suffering—only the vast emptiness of a universe with no future.

"**This is the truth, Davros.**" The creature's voice was a whisper now, soft as a death rattle. "**No matter what you choose, it will end the same. You can't escape your fate. You can't escape *this*.**"

Uno Nguyen © 2024

The visions spun faster and faster, crashing into each other like waves, until Davros felt his mind begin to splinter under the weight of them. Time was folding in on itself. Space was collapsing. He could see all the possible futures, all the broken paths of his life, like a shattered kaleidoscope. And they all led to the same place. The same endless, crushing void.

The forest lashed out, its roots curling around his legs, pulling him down into the earth. The ground seemed to twist, distorting reality itself. His head throbbed with unbearable pain. The voices, the whispers, the visions—they were all melding together, becoming one cacophonous roar.

Davros collapsed to his knees, his vision fading, his breath ragged. His mind was cracking. He had always known that he was nothing more than a pawn in a greater game, but now... now he could feel it. He was just another cog in an endless, pointless cycle.

"What am I fighting for?" he screamed into the void, his voice breaking.

There was no answer. Only silence.

The planet was dying.

Davros could feel it. The ground beneath his feet was trembling, the air crackling with raw energy, and the sky itself seemed to scream in silent agony. The Necron Monolith loomed before him, a towering monolithic structure of cold, mechanical perfection. Its surface shimmered with energy, its presence felt deep in his chest, like a heavy weight pressing down on his bones.

But he was no longer afraid. No, that part of him had died long ago.

He had been broken, twisted, and remade. The artefact within him—once a foreign intrusion—was now a part of him. It pulsed with power, its energy flowing through his veins, fusing with his very flesh. Every nerve screamed in agony, every breath felt like fire, but still he pushed on. The Overlord had to die.

Uno Nguyen © 2024

The Necron Overlord stood before him, its face a mask of ancient, emotionless arrogance. Its cold, metallic form gleamed in the dim light, and its voice echoed in the stillness of the crumbling world.

"You are nothing, human," the Overlord's voice boomed, its tone detached, as if Davros were a mere nuisance. "You are merely a vessel—a puppet. And when the last of your life force drains away, I will be waiting. Just as I have waited for countless millennia."

Davros gritted his teeth, his eyes burning with fury. His body was no longer entirely his own. The corruption from the artefact, the Warp's twisted influence, and the Necron technology had made him into something else—a hybrid of flesh and metal, a living nightmare. But in that moment, as he stared at the Overlord, he understood. It wasn't the Overlord that was the true enemy. It wasn't the Necrons, the Chaos Gods, or even the Rubicon Corporation.

It was himself.

He was the puppet. Always had been. But if he was going to die, he would die on his own terms. He would not bow to fate. He would not serve their twisted designs.

With a roar, Davros reached for the artefact embedded deep within his chest. His fingers dug into the cold, alien metal, feeling its hum beneath his skin. The energy surged within him, responding to his rage, to his defiance. He could feel the Monolith's core—a twisting, unstable force—and he knew what needed to be done.

He had no time to think. No time for hesitation.

Davros slammed his hands into the base of the Monolith, the artefact's energy flaring up in his body, crackling like lightning. His flesh burned as the Necron technology within him merged with the alien device, syncing with the Monolith's power. Sparks flew, and the Monolith trembled, its massive structure vibrating as though something deep inside it was beginning to break apart.

"No…" the Overlord hissed, its eyes narrowing as it stepped forward. "You are making a mistake."

Davros didn't listen. He pushed harder, shoving the artefact deeper into the heart of the Monolith, feeling the energy race through him. His body felt as though it were being torn apart, the fabric of his soul unraveling, but he didn't care. Not anymore. He was past caring.

The Monolith's core was destabilizing.

And then, it happened.

A deafening explosion tore through the air. The Monolith's core exploded in a violent burst of energy, a shockwave of raw, chaotic power that shattered the ground beneath Davros's feet. The explosion ripped through the landscape, throwing rocks and debris into the air, shattering the planet's surface. The sky darkened as the planet's crust began to crack and split, its core imploding under the stress of the unleashed power.

Davros was thrown back, his body crashing into the ground, his senses overwhelmed by the blast. The pain was unbearable. His flesh was searing, his body reshaping itself, the alien technology within him pushing him further from humanity with every passing second. He could feel his thoughts slowing, his mind splintering as the power of the artefact surged within him, trying to take control.

The Overlord was gone. The Monolith was destroyed. The planet was dying.

But Davros had no time to celebrate. He had no victory to claim.

The ground shook violently, and the sky above him erupted into a storm of fire and ash. The planet, its core shattered by the explosion, was collapsing in on itself. The dying world groaned, its surface ripping open, great chasms forming as the planet itself began to tear apart, consumed by the same energy that had just destroyed the Monolith.

Davros crawled to his feet, his mind a blur of pain and rage. His body was no longer his. The Necron and Warp-tainted modifications had accelerated his transformation. His limbs were becoming more machine than man, his thoughts growing distant, as if he were losing himself to the chaos within him.

And he knew, deep down, that he was.

The voices in his head—those maddening whispers—were growing louder, more insistent. They had always been there, but now they were louder, clearer. The Necron Overlords. The Chaos Gods. The echoes of the Warp. All of them were inside him. All of them were pulling him in different directions, and he couldn't fight it anymore.

As the planet began to crumble around him, Davros looked up into the chaos, his eyes burning with fury, his soul torn between the destruction he had wrought and the horrors he was becoming.

He had destroyed the Monolith. He had ended the Overlord.

But what had it cost him?

"This isn't victory," he whispered, his voice hoarse, lost in the roar of the crumbling world. "It's the end."

With that, the ground cracked beneath his feet, and the world around him began to fall apart. The screams of the dying planet echoed in his ears, and in that final moment, Davros realized the truth:

He had never been the one in control.

The Warp was always in control.

And it was consuming him.

THE NEXUS OF FLESH

The first thing Davros noticed upon waking was the hum. It wasn't the steady drone of a machine or the low buzz of an engine. It was something… other. Something alive. The faint vibrations of the ship beneath him seemed to pulse with a rhythm that wasn't entirely natural.

His head throbbed, a dull ache that spread down his neck, down into his augmented body. His chest, his arms, his legs—all of it felt alien to him now. Not quite human, not quite machine. The pain was constant, gnawing at the edges of his awareness, but he had long since grown accustomed to it.

But now, the pain seemed to pulse in time with the hum of the ship, and that… unsettled him.

Davros opened his eyes.

The first thing he saw was the Aeldari. There were three of them. Tall, slender, their features sharp and beautiful, with eyes that gleamed with unnatural intelligence. But beauty could never mask the cold, calculating way they looked at him—like a prize beast in a cage. They stood in a semi-circle around him, their eerie, otherworldly forms draped in flowing, intricate armor.

Uno Nguyen © 2024

He was strapped to a cold, metallic table, the surface hard and unyielding beneath him. It was not the first time he had been restrained—hell, he couldn't remember a time when he wasn't—but the weight of their gaze made him uneasy.

One of the Aeldari spoke. Her voice was musical, but there was no warmth in it.

"You should not be alive," she said, her tone clipped, as if she were stating a fact rather than making an observation. Her fingers—pale and slender—hovered over the intricate controls beside her, tapping them delicately. The ship, it seemed, was alive with her every movement. "The Rubicon's experiments should have been impossible. A creature like you should not exist."

Davros didn't respond at first. His head was spinning. The Warp was all around him, pressing in from the edges of his perception, warping the air itself, bending the very fabric of reality. His eyes flicked from one Aeldari to another, as if trying to gauge which one might make the first move. But their expressions were unreadable, their minds locked behind walls of stone.

The second Aeldari spoke next, his voice softer, less certain. "We cannot simply destroy him. The Rubicon and the Necron... they are threats we cannot ignore. If he has truly been infected by their machines, he may hold the key to unlocking a weapon against them."

The first Aeldari—her lips curling slightly, the slightest smile playing at the edge of her mouth—laughed softly, the sound like the chiming of distant bells.

"And what of the danger to *us*? If we do nothing, he may become their puppet. Or worse." She eyed Davros, her gaze sharp as a blade. "He is not just a man. He is a nexus. Flesh and machine. He carries within him the corruption of both the Necron and the Warp." She leaned closer to him, her eyes narrowing with disdain. "And I will not be the one to fall to *that*."

Davros tried to sit up, but his body refused. His limbs felt as if they were bound by invisible chains, pulling him back into the table. He could feel the ship's pulse thrum through the metal, resonating deep in his bones.

"Enough," the third Aeldari said, her voice cutting through the tension like a razor. "We will use him, but we must move quickly. The longer he is allowed to remain in his current state, the more he becomes... unpredictable."

Their debate continued, but Davros wasn't listening anymore. His mind was elsewhere.

As the Warp bled through the walls of the ship, fragments of memories, nightmares, and visions began to haunt him. The hull of the vessel flickered, rippling as though the very ship itself was warping in and out of reality. One moment, he was in a sterile lab, observing the grotesque experiments of the Rubicon Corporation. The next, he was standing in a burning city, flames licking at the sky, with monstrous shadows looming over the horizon. He could hear the voice of Dr. Celeste Thorn, cold and dismissive, as if she were still watching him from the shadows.

"You were never meant to survive this," she had said.

A shiver ran down his spine.

But then the ship *shifted* again, and everything changed. The walls seemed to twist, and the air itself grew thick with something *unnatural*. The voices of the Aeldari faded into a distant hum as the ship's crew—what little remained of them—screamed in agony.

A rending sound filled the air, the impossible screech of metal twisting against metal. The Aeldari, momentarily distracted, turned toward the sound. Davros could see it—*something* moving outside, clawing at the hull of the vessel, dragging the ship itself into the gaping maw of the Warp.

He heard the scream of one of the Aeldari crew as her body was ripped from the floor, dragged upward as though by invisible hands, her flesh disintegrating in an instant as it was torn from her bones. She vanished into the rift, her scream echoing in every direction before it was snuffed out entirely.

The ship's lights flickered. The air grew thicker with the presence of something else—something older, something hungry.

The Aeldari in front of him seemed unfazed, but Davros could feel the pressure in his head building. It was as if the ship itself was alive, and it was fighting to hold back the oncoming storm.

More crew members were taken. Their bodies twisted and warped, as though the ship itself were transforming them into something else—something that didn't belong in this reality. Twisted shapes, human and alien, seemed to emerge from the walls, flickering in and out of existence, as if the fabric of reality was breaking apart around him.

The Warp had come for them.

And worse, *it had come for him.*

In that instant, his mind cracked wide open.

Visions flooded him: blood and fire, metal and flesh, a galaxy burning beneath his feet. The voices of the Chaos Gods whispered to him, their voices rising in unison as though they were all speaking through him.

The Aeldari were screaming, now. He could hear their voices, high-pitched with terror, as they were consumed by the dark tide. The ship groaned and shuddered, tearing itself apart.

Davros looked around the room, his vision flickering in and out of focus. He could hear the rhythmic hum of the ship, growing more erratic. It was as though it were struggling to hold together, torn between the Warp's influence and the reality it was desperately clinging to.

And then, as the last of the Aeldari crew screamed in agony, their bodies dissolving into nothingness, Davros finally understood.

He wasn't just a weapon. He wasn't just a pawn in some greater game.

He was the nexus.

He was the key.

The ship around him, the Warp itself, the nightmares that danced on the edge of his mind—they all had a purpose. They all led back to him. He was at the center of something far greater than he could comprehend.

And there was no way out.

The world was collapsing again.

It wasn't the kind of collapse that could be measured by the fall of buildings or the tearing apart of flesh. This collapse was deeper, more insidious—one that unraveled the very fabric of reality, pulling everything into the choking, infinite darkness of the Warp. The ship, the Aeldari, the universe itself—everything blurred, all twisted, folding in on itself, until there was nothing left but pain and the echo of a distant scream.

And then the whispers began.

At first, they were faint, like a distant conversation at the edge of hearing. The kind of noise that could be ignored. But soon, they began to sharpen, to grow louder, until they filled his head entirely. Each voice was distinct, yet each spoke with the same venomous accusation.

You are the cause.
You brought this on us.
You betrayed us.

Davros staggered, his mind spinning as the whispers grew into a cacophony of agonized voices. His own name was shouted in the chorus, over and over, like a drumbeat, relentless and suffocating.

He clutched his head, but the voices tore through him, every one a dagger of guilt, every word a wound that could never heal. *Faces. Names.*

He saw them then—his comrades, those who had died because of the Rubicon experiments. Their faces were twisted, deformed by the violence of their deaths. Each one had once been his friend, his team, his responsibility. Now, they were nothing but spirits, hovering in the void of the Warp, their bodies rotting and decayed. They reached for him, their skeletal hands groping, their eyes hollow with accusation.

Sergeant Kellan—his face unrecognizable, his body shredded by the explosion of a Necron device.
Lieutenant Riva—her chest caved in by the weight of a collapsing ceiling.
Private Darnell—his limbs twisted grotesquely as he was absorbed into the Warp, his final scream frozen on his lips.

"Davros!" The voice of Kellan rang out, a hollow, echoing bellow that vibrated the very air around him. *"You promised us survival. You promised us freedom."*

The others echoed his words, their voices merging into a single, seething chorus.

"You gave us death!"

Davros staggered back, the weight of their accusations pressing down on him. His body—half-machine, half-man—twitched as if trying to escape, but there was no escape from this place. He was trapped in their guilt, in the endless spiral of their judgment. His augmented limbs seemed to fight against him, as though they had a mind of their own, rebelling at the sight of the disfigured corpses of his comrades.

"You failed us," Lieutenant Riva's voice cut through his thoughts, sharp and unforgiving. *"We died for your mistakes. For your ambition."*

"*No...*" Davros whispered, but the words felt foreign to him, as if they didn't belong to his mouth. The weight of the accusations, the faces of the dead, it all crashed down on him like an avalanche. "*I didn't—*"

But they were relentless.

"*You let them die!*" The voice of Private Darnell, ragged and twisted, shrieked into his mind. "*You let us all die! You thought you were better than us—*"

Davros recoiled as if struck, his hand shooting up to cover his ears. He wanted to shut them out, but there was no way to silence the barrage. Their accusations were truth, and with every word, the reality of their deaths came flooding back, replaying in excruciating detail.

The explosion in the lab—the bright light, the violent force that had torn through Kellan and the others.
The collapse of the station—the screeching metal, the darkness that swallowed Riva whole.
The moment Darnell had been sucked into the Warp—the agonized expression on his face as his body was twisted and stretched beyond recognition.

It was my fault.

The thought hit him like a hammer to the chest, and in that moment, the pain was too much to bear. He fell to his knees, his breath ragged, choking on the guilt that burned in his chest like a firestorm.

And then the creature appeared.

It was a figure that seemed to emerge from the Warp itself—a towering, inhuman form that flickered and shifted, its very shape defying logic. The edges of its body crackled with Warp energy, and as it stepped closer to him, the air grew colder, darker. The creature's eyes were nothing but endless black voids, and its presence was suffocating, like an inescapable weight pressing on his soul.

It spoke, and its voice was a chorus of all the whispers, every tortured soul, every spirit that had condemned him. But there was something else behind it—a power, an authority that made Davros' augmented body tremble.

"You stand before the Emperor's wrath."

Davros looked up, his mind spinning as the creature's words tore through his thoughts. The Emperor's wrath? He was *nothing* before that power. He was not worthy of the wrath of such an entity—he was not worthy of anything but death.

The creature took another step forward, and the ground beneath him seemed to crack, the Warp itself boiling and twisting. *"You have spilled blood, Davros. You have slaughtered in the name of progress, in the name of your own deluded ambition. Now, you shall answer for it."*

His mind screamed for a way out. But there was no escape. Not from the Warp, not from his actions, not from the consequences of his every choice.

The creature raised a hand, and the forms of his fallen comrades emerged from the shadows once more. Kellan, Riva, Darnell—all of them, their broken bodies looming over him like a judgment too great to escape.

And in the creature's voice, he could hear the harsh, unforgiving tone of the Emperor himself, as though every word had been spoken by the man whose name he had once worshipped. The figure stepped closer still, the pressure in the air becoming unbearable.

"Defend yourself, Davros," it growled, its voice carrying a promise of pain. *"Or perish."*

Davros's pulse quickened, his senses overwhelmed by the spectral images of his comrades, the creature's terrible presence, the unrelenting weight of his guilt. He was pulled into a battle, not of flesh and steel, but of his mind. Of his very soul.

Kellan's face warped, his mouth stretching into a twisted grin as he advanced, his fingers sharp like claws. Riva, too, reached for him, her body flickering as if she were made of smoke. Darnell's disfigured visage twisted, his mouth stretching wide in a silent scream.

Davros fought, struggling to hold on to what little sanity he had left. He had nothing left but rage—the only thing that had kept him going since he had first started this descent. Rage, and a terrible, gnawing hunger for answers.

"I didn't *want* this!" he screamed, his voice breaking, his augmented hands trembling.

But no one answered. The creature stepped closer, the ground beneath him trembling as the twisted forms of his fallen comrades reached for him.

In that moment, everything—every mistake, every loss, every betrayal—came crashing down on him like the weight of a thousand worlds.

And as the vision of Kellan's face morphed into a grotesque mockery of his own, Davros realized there was no escaping the truth.

He had always been the architect of his own ruin.

The ground beneath Davros' boots was unstable, shifting in a way that made him question if he was truly standing at all. It wasn't the kind of instability that came from an earthquake or the tremors of a collapsing building. This was something deeper, something rooted in the fabric of reality itself. He was standing on a plane where the boundaries of time and space didn't exist, where the very laws of physics bent and snapped like brittle twigs.

The Nexus.

Uno Nguyen © 2024

This place—this surreal convergence of infinite realities—was a nexus of untold power. The Warp stretched out before him like an endless abyss, its swirling tides of dark energy beckoning, twisting, and distorting everything around him. Flickers of alternate worlds, both terrifying and beautiful, flared in and out of view like fractured mirrors. The air shimmered with the weight of something vast, something ancient.

In the distance, he could see the shadows of battles fought across impossible landscapes. The ground was littered with corpses—some human, some not. The clash of metallic and psychic forces filled the air with a constant, thunderous hum, a cacophony of destruction that rattled his bones. This was a battlefield, but not in the traditional sense. It was a war between realities. Between gods.

And in the midst of it all, Davros stood, his body crackling with unnatural energy. The artefact buried deep within his chest thrummed, a pulsing heartbeat of malignancy. As he moved forward, the Warp reacted to him, rippling with an ominous energy, as though it recognized him, acknowledged his presence.

The Nexus had been waiting for him.

At that moment, he realized the full weight of the truth that had been revealed to him—he was not a mere player in this struggle. He was the key. The artefact inside him, fused with his body and soul, had opened a gateway to this place. His very existence was now bound to the Nexus. And if anyone was going to wield its power, it would be him.

The air began to warp and distort further. He saw flashes of armies, colossal and monstrous, converging from all sides. The forces of Chaos, twisted daemons of every kind, surged forward in a flood of warp-born rage. Their shapes flickered like half-formed dreams, each one more nightmarish than the last. The Necron constructs, pale and implacable, marched in perfect, mechanical precision, their cold, alien minds calculating every move. And the Aeldari—aloof and enigmatic—watched from the shadows, their glowing eyes fixed on the prize they had longed for.

They had all come for the Nexus. For the power it contained. And for the one who would control it.

"He's here."

The voice pierced the air like a knife through flesh. It was not a voice—more like a collective chorus, a thousand voices blending into one. But it was not just any voice. It was the voice of a god. The voice of the Chaos Gods themselves.

They had been waiting.

The ground shook violently as Davros staggered forward, his vision swimming with impossible sights. The sky above was a whirlpool of colors and shapes, like the very fabric of reality was tearing apart at the seams. Somewhere, far off in the distance, he could hear the sound of trumpets blaring, and the war cries of daemon legions.

"Davros..." The voice again, this time more insistent. *"You are the bridge between worlds. You are the one who will decide the fate of the galaxy."*

He gritted his teeth, feeling the oppressive weight of their eyes, even though he could not see them. It was as if the Warp itself were watching him—pressing in on him, suffocating him.

The shadows before him shifted, and from them emerged a figure—tall, impossibly slender, draped in dark robes that seemed to flow into the very fabric of the Nexus. The figure's face was obscured by a hood, but its presence was unmistakable.

Aeldari. The mysterious, enigmatic race whose eyes burned with ancient knowledge and unknowable intentions.

The figure raised a hand, and the air around it shimmered with psychic power. "The Nexus will fall into the hands of the worthy," the Aeldari said, its voice cold and detached. "And you, Davros, are nothing but a tool."

Uno Nguyen © 2024

Davros' hand twitched at his side, but the artefact inside him burned with a painful intensity, urging him to respond. He was not a tool. He had never been a tool. He had *been* the tool, but no longer.

The Aeldari's smile was a flash of cruel amusement. "You think you can control this power? The Nexus is a living thing, and you—*you*—are nothing but a catalyst."

With that, the figure extended its hand toward him, and the very air around Davros began to warp, as if the Nexus itself was bending to the will of the Aeldari. The ground beneath him cracked and splintered as a thousand hands of pure psychic force reached out, grasping at him, pulling him down into the depths of the Warp.

He could hear the whispers again, louder than ever before. The voices of the dead, the voices of the gods, the voices of the universe itself.

But there was no time for fear.

In that instant, Davros could feel the power surge within him, the power of the artefact, the power of the Nexus. He no longer cared about being used. He no longer cared about the weight of his past.

The only thing that mattered was *this*. The moment of truth.

With a roar, Davros reached out, his body warping further, flesh and metal twisting into something far beyond human. The Nexus *responded* to him. It thrummed, vibrating with unimaginable energy, as if it recognized him as its true master.

The battle unfolded before him in a violent explosion of power. Soldiers—both human and alien—clashed in a frenzy of carnage. The Necron constructs unleashed their cold, calculating fury, while the daemons of Chaos tore through the battlefield, howling with bloodlust. Aeldari warriors danced like shadows, their blades flashing through the air with deadly grace.

But none of them mattered. Not anymore.

Davros was at the center, the fulcrum upon which this war would balance. The Nexus pulsed with his every movement, every heartbeat, every breath.

And then, as if all the forces of the universe had gathered to focus upon him, the Nexus reacted to Davros' will. A blinding light erupted from within him, a light so intense that it tore through the battlefield, scattering all those around him like dust in the wind.

The moment stretched, timeless, as the power of the Warp and the fabric of reality itself bent to his will.

This was his moment.

And in the center of it all, Davros whispered to himself, barely audible over the roar of the battle:

"This is how it ends."

The Nexus was collapsing.

Davros could feel it in his bones, in the very blood coursing through his veins. The energy that had once thrummed with power, guiding his every step, now twisted and churned like a living thing in agony. The Warp itself seemed to convulse, its malevolent energy warping the very fabric of space and time around him. The whispers, once muffled and distant, now howled in his ears like a storm of tortured souls, each one trying to drown out the other, each one clawing at his mind.

The visions began as flashes, brief moments of clarity in a sea of madness. He saw himself—no, not himself, but something worse, something beyond human. His body was a grotesque mockery of flesh and metal, towering over a galaxy of burning worlds. Stars bled out of existence as his hand reached down, crushing entire systems in a single motion. The screams of the billions who perished at his command echoed in the distance, faint and distant, like the wailing of lost souls trapped in the void.

Uno Nguyen © 2024

This is your future, the voices whispered, *your destiny. You were always meant to rule, Davros. You are the next step in the evolution of the universe.*

He tried to tear his eyes away from the visions, but they clung to him, suffocating him in their weight. His body, once a tool of the Rubicon Corporation, now seemed to pulse with the energy of the Nexus itself, a living conduit for the Warp's terrible power. His mind fractured further as the visions grew more vivid, more detailed.

He saw himself sitting upon a throne of skulls, a dark god over a ruined galaxy. His every word a command that the galaxy would bow to. His eyes—no longer human—burned with the madness of the Chaos Gods. The vision was beautiful and terrible all at once. The universe was his playground, and every life, every soul, was his to control.

But it was a nightmare. A lie.

And it was not a future he wanted.

The air around him shimmered with the cold presence of the Chaos Gods. Their voices boomed inside his skull, an overwhelming cacophony that threatened to drown him. The ground beneath his feet cracked open, revealing swirling chasms of dark energy, as if the very world were being undone by their power.

Embrace your power, Davros, Khorne's voice rumbled, thick with bloodlust. *Bask in the rivers of blood, and carve a throne from the skulls of your enemies. You were always meant to rule with an iron fist.*

No! Davros screamed inwardly. *I am not like you!*

Do not reject your power, Slaanesh's voice coiled around him like a sweet poison. *Release yourself from the shackles of pain. Let the ecstasy of the Warp wash over you. You could be free, if only you surrender to me.*

Davros felt his hands tremble, his body flickering between the realms of reality and the Warp. The artefact within him pulsed with unbearable intensity, resonating with the energies of the Chaos Gods.

Peace awaits you, Davros, Nurgle's voice whispered softly, like a father coaxing his child to sleep. *Join me, and I will give you a place of eternal rest. No more pain. No more fear.*

I will not! Davros shouted, his mind shaking from the weight of the voices. *I refuse!*

Then, from the darkness, a familiar presence stepped forward—a figure that towered above him like a nightmare made flesh. The Necron Overlord, its gaunt face locked in a grin of cruel amusement, stood before him once more.

So, you resist, the Overlord's voice crackled, like metal scraping against metal. *You think you can escape your fate, Davros?*

It raised one skeletal hand, and the visions flared brighter, more vivid, more agonizing. Davros saw himself again—his monstrous form, crushing worlds underfoot. Entire cities turned to ash, their populations snuffed out in an instant. He could see his own reflection in the eyes of his victims—twisted, horrific, unstoppable. He was everything he had sworn to destroy.

The Overlord laughed, its hollow voice filled with disdain. *You are nothing more than a tool, a vessel for the power of the Nexus. You will become the monster you hate, and you will enjoy every moment of it. The galaxy will burn, and you will be its architect.*

Davros' body shook with fury. His eyes burned with hatred as the Overlord's cruel laughter echoed in his ears. This was the endgame. This was what they wanted him to become.

But no.

I will not be your slave! Davros roared, his voice cutting through the maelstrom of madness. *I'll destroy it all before I become your slave!*

Uno Nguyen © 2024

The Nexus trembled. His body rippled with raw, unrestrained power. The artefact within him howled, a sound like a thousand voices screaming for release. The Warp tore open around him, dark tendrils of energy lashing at the edges of his consciousness. His body was no longer his own; it was a weapon of unimaginable power, a conduit between the physical and the Warp, an avatar of destruction.

Davros turned his gaze to the Overlord, his eyes filled with pure defiance. *You were wrong about me,* he whispered, his voice a cold, bitter thing. *I will not be the instrument of your destruction. I will be the one to end this.*

He raised his hands, and the very fabric of reality shuddered in response. He could feel the Nexus quaking beneath him, as if it were alive, torn between its desire to enslave him and his will to destroy it.

I will be the last voice in this void, Davros muttered, his voice growing louder as the power of the Warp surged through him. *And this galaxy will burn in the fires of its own making.*

The ground split open, and the sky above him cracked, torn apart by the energy of his will. A storm of psychic power unleashed itself, a cascade of destruction that sent shockwaves through the Nexus.

And as the world around him crumbled, Davros realized that there was no turning back.

The Nexus had become a singularity, a swirling storm of energies so chaotic, so beyond understanding, that it seemed to tear the very fabric of reality asunder. Every force that had ever existed, every power that had ever sought to control the universe, was converging here, in this moment of destruction. Davros could feel it all—the weight of the Rubicon Corporation, the weight of the Necrons, the weight of the Chaos Gods, all pressing in on him. And through it all, there was only one thing left for him to do: *End it.*

His body, once human, now a grotesque hybrid of flesh and metal, trembled with the sheer power coursing through it. He could feel the Nexus—its energies, its destructive potential—calling to him, waiting for his command. His mind, fragmented and broken, grasped at fleeting memories of what he once was. Before the artefact, before the madness, before all of this.

He remembered the first time he had held the artefact, so long ago. He remembered the promise of power, of progress, of control. And now, all of it felt hollow. The power he had craved, the legacy he had thought to leave, was nothing more than a lie. The Nexus was a prison, and he had become both its architect and its prisoner.

He could feel the Chaos Gods watching him, their malignant presences a constant hum in the back of his mind. *Embrace your fate, Davros. Become the master of all,* they whispered, their voices laced with both temptation and mockery. But he could no longer hear them. The whispers of the Warp, the promises of immortality, the endless call of the Necron Overlords—all of it faded into nothingness.

He had made his choice. He would not be their pawn.

With a scream that was part rage, part sorrow, Davros raised his arms, and the Nexus responded. The very air around him seemed to tear, the Warp shuddering violently in response to his defiance. Energy arced from his body, crackling like a storm, the power of the artefact unleashed in full force. He felt it all—every heartbeat, every cell, every ounce of energy he had left in his body. The Nexus was collapsing, and he would be the one to destroy it.

No more.

The ground beneath him cracked open, the sky above him shattered into a million pieces, and the very laws of reality bent and broke under the weight of his actions. Time itself unraveled, twisting into impossible loops, as the explosion of psychic energy engulfed the Nexus. The Rubicon Corporation, the Necron Overlords, the Chaos Gods—all of them, reduced to nothing in a single, overwhelming moment of annihilation.

Uno Nguyen © 2024

For the briefest of moments, Davros felt… peace. No voices, no whispers, no taunts. Just the pure, raw silence of the void. He was alone. And yet, somehow, he was not.

His body began to dissolve. Flesh and metal peeled away like dying leaves in the wind, and the core of the artefact—now a part of him—sizzled and crackled, its energies spiraling out of control. His limbs, once strong and augmented, began to crumble, turning to ash and bone, the process of his unmaking slow and agonizing.

But the pain, strange as it was, did not matter. Nothing mattered anymore. He was beyond the reach of the Gods, beyond the reach of the universe itself. He was falling into the void, into the darkness where time and space no longer held sway.

And through the fog of his fading consciousness, a single thought persisted.

I was Davros. But I am no longer.

The last remnants of his human form crumbled, disintegrating into the Warp, as if he were being erased from existence itself. And yet, as his body dissolved and his thoughts scattered like dust in the wind, there was a final, haunting realization that twisted his fading mind.

I have become nothing… and everything.

THE VOID ETERNAL

The void was an endless abyss, stretching infinitely in every direction. No stars, no galaxies, no horizons—just a crushing, oppressive darkness that seemed to swallow everything whole. Time was irrelevant here, moments slipping through his fingers like sand, each one twisting and warping into something else. Memories, feelings, images, all mixed together into a blurring haze, a maddening swirl of confusion. He could no longer tell where he ended and where the void began.

For a fleeting instant, he thought he saw his own reflection— a twisted, mutilated version of himself, staring back from the darkness. His body was still incomplete, parts of it shifting and changing, flesh merging with metal, organs fusing with circuitry. But the reflection was wrong—there was something missing, something *more* than just the physical transformation. His soul felt absent, hollowed out, consumed by the very forces he had tried to control.

And then, as if the void itself had heard his thoughts, the whispers began again.

Davros… the voices purred, soft and taunting, seeping into his mind like poison. *Do you remember? Can you still feel what it was like to be human? To have purpose?*

He staggered in place, clutching at his head as the voices grew louder, more insistent. They were all around him now, a cacophony of twisted mockery, each one pulling him deeper into the abyss. The Chaos Gods had found him, and they were not done with him yet.

Khorne's blood spills, but yours is nothing.
Slaanesh's pleasure fades, yet your pain is endless.
Nurgle's decay is eternal, and so are you.
Tzeentch's schemes are eternal, just as your futile resistance is.

The voices wrapped themselves around his mind, like a dozen hands squeezing tighter and tighter, pushing him toward the brink of madness. He saw fragments of his past—faces of comrades long dead, the cruel experiments he had conducted, the broken soldiers, the agony of those he had betrayed—and they all turned on him, accusing him, screaming his name in fury and sorrow.

You were nothing before the Rubicon.
You are nothing now.
You will always be nothing.

The weight of their words crushed him. He fought it, tried to reject them, but it was no use. The more he resisted, the more they flooded his mind, every thought slipping further away, every memory decaying until it was a ghost of what it once was. *You chose this,* they whispered. *You chose power. You chose to destroy. And for what?*

The visions of his past twisted and contorted—his first awakening to the artefact, the hope he had once felt in its potential, the promises of immortality and control. But it was all a lie. The artefact had never been his to command. It was an anchor, chaining him to this endless, collapsing reality. The universe was not his to bend; it had broken him long ago.

Uno Nguyen © 2024

He fell to his knees in the void, his breath ragged and broken, as the Chaos Gods' laughter rang in his ears.

You cannot escape us, Davros. Not here. Not ever.

The words echoed endlessly, reverberating through his shattered consciousness. He closed his eyes, feeling his last human thoughts slip away. There was nothing left. No redemption. No escape. No purpose.

You will never be free.

His body, now a twisted mockery of life, quivered in the darkness as his mind began to fragment beyond repair. The past, the present, and the future all collided into a single, inescapable truth: he was nothing more than a tool, a puppet, a sacrifice. All that he had done, all the horrors he had wrought—meaningless. The universe had chewed him up and spit him out. His existence had been nothing but a passing ripple in the grand tide of the Warp. A futile struggle in the face of cosmic indifference.

The Chaos Gods were right. He had *always* been nothing.

And as he sank further into the abyss, all he could feel was the overwhelming weight of his own insignificance.

The Warp stretched before him, an unbroken expanse of starlit void and fractal chaos. It was a place beyond all comprehension, where time folded in on itself, and the rules of reality were twisted like taffy. Davros floated, disoriented, his senses splintered by the countless voices of the Warp that clawed at his mind. The familiar voices of the Chaos Gods were absent, replaced by something darker, more insidious. Something *older*.

He couldn't see them, but he could feel them—unseen eyes pressing down on him, their cold gaze sinking into his very soul. The sense of being watched, of being *known*, of being an object of study, gripped him like a vise. His body, now a grotesque patchwork of flesh and metal, pulsed with the unholy energy of the Warp. Every cell, every nerve screamed with the weight of his transformation, but it was more than that. Something *else* was inside him now—something that controlled him.

The voices began, faint at first, like the hum of a far-off star. But soon, they coalesced into words—thousands of voices speaking at once, too many to make sense of, and yet their meaning was unmistakable.

"Davros..."

His name rang through the Warp like a bell tolling in the dead of night. He staggered in the emptiness, trying to push the voices out, but they burrowed deeper into his mind.

"We have watched you, Davros. We have seen your every step, your every mistake. You are ours."

He recoiled, but the voices pressed on, surrounding him, binding him in invisible chains. His breath quickened, panic rising in his chest. *No... this can't be real. This isn't happening. I—*

"We are the Watchers, Davros. The architects of your existence. The ones who shaped your every thought, your every action."

His heart thudded in his chest as the realization hit him like a bolt of lightning. He tried to scream, but no sound escaped his lips. His entire life, every decision he had made, every atrocity he had committed—it had all been part of their design. He had never been in control. They had always been there, waiting, watching.

"You thought the Necrons, the Rubicon Corporation, the Chaos Gods were your adversaries. But we were always the true force pulling the strings."

Davros staggered backward in the dark, a sickening realization flooding through him. The artefact that had infected his body, the transformation that had twisted him into this thing—he had *never* been meant to be its master. He had been *chosen*, but not for his power, not for his strength. He had been chosen to be their *puppet*.

Uno Nguyen © 2024

"All the pain you have caused, all the destruction... it was not your doing. It was our will."

The blackness around him shifted, flickering like the pulse of a dying star, and then visions began to unfold before him. He saw them—alien civilizations, vast and powerful, brought low by forces far beyond their understanding. The Tyranids, endless in number and hunger, devouring entire worlds. The Orks, led by warbosses whose brutal might was bent to a purpose beyond even their reckoning. The T'au, their empire of unity and peace, manipulated into endless conflict.

"All were prey. All were led into the jaws of the abyss. And you, Davros, you were the key to opening it. You were the perfect vessel for our hunger."

He saw himself now—twisted, broken, an instrument of chaos. His mind fractured into a thousand pieces as the enormity of what he had become, what he had always *been*, sank in. His body, his soul, his mind—they were not his own. They had been shaped, altered, twisted to serve the Watchers' purpose.

"We have given you the gift of seeing all things, Davros. The power to reshape the universe. To be the harbinger of the end. And we have fed on your suffering, on your doubt, on your rage."

The more he struggled, the tighter the noose of their influence became. His every action, every thought, was like an offering to them, feeding their insatiable hunger. His failure, his pain, his torment—it had all been part of their grand design.

"You are not the master of your fate, Davros. You were never meant to be. You are a tool, a pawn in a game too vast for you to understand."

The visions grew more vivid, more grotesque. He saw himself—still alive, still breathing, still fighting—but broken, shattered, a hollow shell of what he once was. A puppet, strung along by invisible hands, dancing to the tune of the Watchers' whims. His body—no longer human—twisted further, grotesquely, its once-organic parts overtaken by alien technology and Warp corruption. He felt his mind splintering, his thoughts consumed by a deep, gnawing despair.

"This is your purpose, Davros. This is your truth."

He tried to scream, tried to fight back, but the words refused to leave his throat. Every fiber of his being screamed for release, but there was none. No salvation. No redemption.

"You have no escape. You belong to us, Davros. Now and forever."

And then, before him, eyes appeared—thousands of them, blinking and bleeding, eyes that were not eyes, but something more. They stared at him, filled with ancient malice, with a hunger that could never be sated. Their gaze burned through him, seeing everything. *All of him.*

"We have always been watching. And now, Davros, we will feast on you as we have feasted on countless others."

His voice faltered, his chest heaving with the weight of the truth. He had always known, deep down. That no matter what he did, no matter how far he pushed, how much power he sought, he would always be just another pawn in a much larger game.

"I am not your puppet!"

But the words felt empty. Hollow. A desperate cry for something that would never come. He had no power left. He had been broken, used, discarded. And now, they were here to consume the last remnants of him.

The Watchers' laughter filled the void, a sound like the crackling of ancient bones, like the shriek of a thousand souls lost in darkness. He tried to fight it. He tried to claw at the walls of his mind, but the more he struggled, the tighter their hold became.

His voice, weak and trembling, broke through the dark, but it was too late.

Uno Nguyen © 2024

"I... I am not yours…"

But the Watchers only smiled, and the last shred of his defiance slipped away.

The dark of the Warp pressed in from all sides, thick and suffocating. Yet, in the suffocating blackness, there was a light—cold, distant, unknowable. The Watchers' eyes, those thousands of writhing, bleeding pupils, were still there, hovering at the edge of his consciousness. They had granted him their gift, and now he was no longer merely Davros. He was something else, something *far beyond*.

The transformation had begun. His body, already mutilated and reformed by the twisted power of the artefact, was no longer his own. Every cell, every molecule, pulsed with unnatural energy. His limbs were stretched, elongated, and reshaped, no longer bound by the laws of flesh and bone. Metal intertwined with muscle, like an insect's exoskeleton, a grotesque hybrid of man and machine. His senses fractured and splintered, and he no longer experienced the world in a linear way.

In an instant, the Warp expanded before him, bending and twisting. He saw the universe not as it was, but as it would inevitably become—decay, entropy, and the slow, inevitable death of all things. He saw stars flicker and die, their light swallowed by the black void. Worlds burned, civilizations rose and fell, all of it meaningless. Nothing endured.

He saw the T'au, their empire of harmony, eroded by the ravages of time, their unity a brittle illusion, consumed by the tide of entropy. He saw the Orks, their endless wars an echo of the void they inhabited, a futile flailing against the inevitable. Even the Imperium, its might and arrogance, a mere speck in the vastness of an uncaring universe, disintegrated to dust, swallowed by the unrelenting decay.

And then, in a moment of terrible clarity, Davros saw himself. He saw his life, his rise to power, his corruption. He saw the

Uno Nguyen © 2024

chaos he had wrought—the Rubicon Corporation, the experiments, the modifications, the monstrosities—and he understood that it had all been for nothing. In the face of the universe's ultimate decay, all of it was meaningless.

"You see it now," whispered the voices of the Watchers, their tones cold, distant, like the sound of a thousand broken stars. *"The truth. There is no meaning, no purpose. All things must wither and die."*

The weight of the revelation crushed him, drove him to his knees in the void. His mind splintered, broken by the vast, unfeeling knowledge that now flooded his consciousness. The universe itself was a great machine of death, grinding everything into nothingness. There was no hope. There was no future. Only an endless, unending collapse.

But the Watchers were not finished. They had more to show him.

Davros' form twisted further, every movement a painful distortion. He felt it—*them*—the Necron tomb worlds, vast, cold, and ancient, stirring at the far edges of the galaxy. The Monoliths hummed with ancient power, their mechanical servants stirring in the depths of their slumber, waiting to awaken. But what were they now? Instruments of death, yes, but also another echo of the same endless cycle. The Necrons, too, were slaves to the void, unable to escape the entropic force that consumed them as well.

But now, Davros was beyond them, beyond the Necrons and the Warp and the Chaos Gods. He could feel them all, like ripples in the fabric of reality. He could sense the cold metallic hearts of the Necrons as they stirred, each vibration a note in the symphony of destruction. He was not just aware of them. He could *feel* them, as if his very essence was a part of the cosmic web that connected everything to the same ultimate fate.

It was no longer terrifying. In fact, it was almost *pleasurable*. There was no fear, no pain. There was only the cold ecstasy of being beyond it all—of being part of the inevitable collapse. He was the *end*, the final note in the symphony of existence, and the knowledge that he was beyond mortality, beyond the constraints of flesh, filled him with a dark, twisted satisfaction.

The Watchers whispered, their voices so vast, so ancient, they seemed to echo from the very bones of the universe itself.

"You are nothing, Davros. And yet, you are everything. You are the end, the beginning, and the void between. You are our creation, and our triumph."

Davros' transformation was complete. His human form—if such a thing could be called human anymore—was gone. His body had become an amalgamation of metal, flesh, and something *else*, something incomprehensible. His senses had multiplied, spiraling outward into realms of perception that no mortal being should ever experience. He felt the vibrations of the universe itself, heard the quiet, agonizing hum of dying stars, and felt the deep, consuming hunger of the void.

He reached out with his new senses, feeling the ripples of existence echoing throughout the Warp and the material universe. His mind, once constrained by mortal limits, now stretched across infinity, touching everything and nothing at once.

But his body—it was no longer flesh. No longer machine. It was a *force*, a distortion in the fabric of reality. He could feel the Necron tombs, the rising tide of the Tyranid swarm, the endless tide of Orks and the fragile, flickering flame of human civilization. All of it was *meaningless*. All of it was *insignificant*.

His hands—if they could even be called hands now— stretched out, claws of metal and shifting flesh, reaching for the infinite darkness.

"I... am the void," he whispered, the words rasping from a throat that no longer existed.

But the truth was in his very being. He was the void, the end of all things. He had been consumed by the Watchers' design, turned into something far worse than human, something far more horrifying. He had become a force of entropy itself, beyond the reach of life, beyond the reach of death.

And yet, in that moment of cosmic clarity, there was no fear. No anguish. Only the vast, echoing silence of the void.

Davros' mind had long since splintered, a fractured mosaic of thoughts and memories that could no longer piece together a coherent reality. He existed now in a space between spaces, drifting through a rift in the fabric of time and matter. The Warp pulsed around him, its endless tides crashing through the blackness like a storm of twisted, screaming souls. Reality itself bent and warped, its very threads unraveling as the Chaos Gods' influence seeped deeper into the universe. Their madness poured out of the rift like oil, slick and consuming, devouring everything it touched.

He watched, helpless, as galaxies burned, their stars flickering out one by one, their systems collapsing into the yawning void. Planets, once teeming with life, were swallowed whole by the tides of the Warp, their inhabitants lost to the madness of the Chaos Gods. In the distance, he saw the last vestiges of human civilization—scattered, broken, fighting to hold on to some semblance of existence on the edges of a dying galaxy. Their ships, once proud and mighty, now burned like fragile embers in the dark.

Davros felt it all—the slow, suffocating weight of the end of everything. The dying gasps of billions of worlds. The screams of the broken, their final cries snuffed out by the endless dark. But more than that, he felt the pull of the Warp, its fingers tightening around him, pulling him deeper into its clutches. His form—no longer entirely human, no longer entirely machine—twisted, writhing in pain as it was slowly consumed by the power he had once sought to wield.

He was nothing but a shard of something vast, an echo of a power he had never truly understood. He had been the weapon, the tool, and now he was the instrument of the universe's annihilation. His very existence had become the catalyst for the slow death of everything. And yet, in the midst of it all, a strange emptiness settled over him. A gnawing, hollow ache that he could not shake.

"Is there truly nothing left for me?" The thought flickered in his mind, fleeting but persistent. It gnawed at him, deep in the recesses of his mind. He had become the end of all things, the destroyer of worlds, the harbinger of a dark, inevitable oblivion. And yet, for all of that power, he felt an emptiness that even the vastness of the Warp could not fill. It was as if he had been hollowed out from the inside, a vessel without purpose or meaning.

There was no hope left, no future to fight for. The Rubicon Corporation had fallen, the last remnants of humanity were dying, and the Chaos Gods—those he had once sought to control—were as helpless against the tide of entropy as the rest of the galaxy. All that remained were shadows, echoes of a time before the universe had torn itself apart.

The Rubicon Spire—the once-great monument to human ambition—was now a decaying husk drifting through the empty void. The hull of the ship groaned, its steel frame warping and bending under the strain of the collapsing reality around it. Davros' mind shifted in and out of focus, the Warp's influence pressing against him, urging him to surrender, to give in to its power. But he resisted, as futile as it was. His soul was no longer his own. It was fragmented, shattered, dissolving into the very fabric of reality itself.

He stood at the heart of the Spire, watching as the last lights of the dying universe flickered out around him. He could see the faint shadows of human souls—those who had once called him leader, those he had betrayed or destroyed—flitting through the corridors of the dying ship. They were mere flickers in the darkness, lost, forgotten. He could hear their voices, though muted, calling to him from the past. Accusations. Pleas for mercy. The faint echoes of lives he had ruined.

"What have I done?" The thought drifted through his mind, but it was lost almost as soon as it arrived, swallowed by the deeper, darker thoughts that crowded his mind. He had been the architect of

his own destruction, and now he was nothing more than a shadow in a dying world. His body, now little more than an abomination of flesh and metal, twisted and writhed in pain, as if seeking some final release. But there was none to be found.

The Warp was no longer just a force he could manipulate. It had become his prison, his tomb, and the tomb of all things. It whispered to him now, not with promises of power, but with the harsh truth of the universe's end. The eternal struggle of the Warp— its endless cycles of death and rebirth—had come to a close. Nothing would rise again. No new gods, no new empires. Only dust.

And still, the emptiness gnawed at him.

"No one survives," Davros whispered to himself, his voice hollow and distant. His words echoed through the empty halls of the Spire, a sad reminder of all he had lost and all that had been lost around him. *"Not even me."*

His body began to flicker, losing its coherence. He could feel the last remnants of his humanity dissolving, slipping through his grasp like sand through an open hand. There was no more Davros. No more human. No more machine. Just the endless void, the inevitable collapse of everything he had ever known.

And still, he felt the pull of the Warp—still, he felt the watchful eyes of the Chaos Gods, still they whispered to him. But their voices were fading now, consumed by the ever-growing darkness. There was no power left to seek. No hope left to grasp.

Only dust and shadows.

In the boundless emptiness, there was no longer any sense of time. No rising or setting of stars. No past, no future. Only the ceaseless, unbroken cycle of suffering and death that the universe had become. The fabric of reality itself had unraveled, its threads scattering into the abyss, leaving nothing behind but a void in which Davros existed as little more than an echo of his former self—a disembodied point of awareness, suspended in the cold, eternal dark.

He could feel the pain. The pain of everything. Every death, every scream, every tear. It was as if the entire universe had become a single, infinite wound, one that never healed, never ceased. And he felt it all—each moment of agony, each flicker of light extinguished in darkness.

The loop was endless. There was no escape. There was only this—this suffocating, unrelenting cycle of creation and destruction, rebirth and annihilation. It was as though every instant in the history of the universe was repeating itself again and again, a never-ending spiral of despair and decay.

He had been here before, had he not?

The Necrons, now fully awakened, moved through the galaxy like a cold, unstoppable tide. Their bodies gleamed with metallic perfection as they harvested the last fragments of life. The stars were snuffed out like candles, and the universe seemed to shrink with each passing moment, each cold step of their march across time. He could feel it, the slow death of everything. The Necron Overlords, once so proud and mighty, now rulers of an empty universe. They ruled over the ashes of civilizations long forgotten, their cold, unfeeling metal hands grasping for something they could no longer hold.

Was it ever any different?

Davros watched in horror as the Aeldari—the once-proud race of seers and warriors—slowly withered, falling into their own extinction, their final cries echoing in the void. The fall of the Aeldari had been inevitable, and now, their fate was sealed. He saw their souls, shattered and broken, trapped in the immensity of the Warp, twisted by the relentless pull of the Chaos Gods. There was no escape for them, not now, not ever.

And the Orks...

Davros had seen their endless wars, their constant fighting. It had all seemed so absurd, so meaningless. And yet now, in the collapsing universe, it was clear—there would never be peace. The Orks, ever destructive, ever aggressive, tore into each other with unrestrained fury. Their wars had no end. No victor. They would fight, and they would die, and the cycle would begin again.

But it didn't stop. It couldn't. The Tyranids came next, their insatiable hunger consuming everything they encountered, devouring what was left of the universe like locusts descending on a barren field. There was no refuge from them. No place to hide. The Tyranids, with their endless swarms and insidious hive minds, consumed the last vestiges of the galaxy, leaving behind only a hushed void.

The T'au, too, were not exempt from the cycle. Their empire, once brimming with ambition and hope, was twisted by the slow, insidious touch of corruption. The purity of their ideals turned to dust, their unity shattered by the growing rot that began to take root within their society. They, too, would fall.

All of them. Gone. Forgotten. Their names, their legacies, erased from the universe.

It was all a game. A cruel joke, and he had played his part.

But Davros could not act. He was powerless. The force that had once driven him to conquer, to reshape the galaxy to his will, was now a distant memory. He could do nothing but watch as the universe he had sought to control collapsed around him, and each cycle began again—infinitely, without end.

He could no longer differentiate between the deaths of others and his own. The screams of the dying became his own. The endless, agonizing pain twisted through his consciousness, suffocating him, breaking him. Every planet's fall was his fall. Every civilization's extinction was his extinction. He could feel them all, the billions upon billions of lives snuffed out in a single, violent instant. Every war, every slaughter. All of it. All of them. His mind shattered under the weight.

"I... I..." The thought started, but it was lost, swallowed by the endless repetition of the void.

Was this what it meant to exist in the end? To feel everything, all at once, without end? Was this what it meant to truly understand the futility of it all?

Davros' awareness flickered, his perception fractured. The pain continued, unrelenting, suffocating. He could no longer separate himself from the suffering, no longer remember who he had been, who he had once been. He had become the pain, the cycle, the eternal witness to destruction.

And yet...

And yet, the worst part was this: there would be no release. No redemption. No salvation. Nothing.

The universe—everything he had ever known, everything he had ever sought to control—was collapsing into oblivion. And he would never, ever escape it.

He was the beginning and the end. The key and the lock. The void and the star. And with one final, excruciating scream, he disappeared into the infinite darkness, his existence fading, lost to the very cycle he had helped create.

THE BLACK HORIZON

The blackness was endless. It stretched beyond comprehension, an infinite chasm of void and decay, where the very fabric of space and time seemed to twist into impossible shapes. What had once been the universe was now a shattered expanse, an astral graveyard of half-formed stars and broken planets. In the distance, the echoes of cosmic storms pulsed like the dying heartbeat of a world that had already passed into oblivion.

Davros, or what remained of him, floated through the remnants of this shattered cosmos. His body—a grotesque and mangled mockery of the man he had once been—was no longer the human form that had once worn his name. It was a grotesque fusion of flesh, metal, and cosmic energy, ever-shifting and warping in the emptiness. His mind, too, was fractured, suspended somewhere between the mortal and the divine, between man and the incomprehensible entities he had once believed he could control.

He felt no physical pain, only a cold, terrible awareness of the horror that was his existence. The Watchers—those ancient, unknowable beings who had twisted his fate and set him on his path of madness—were gone. But their presence lingered, like a poison in the very air he breathed. Their designs had been fulfilled, their game had played out, and Davros was the final pawn left on the board, forgotten and abandoned.

Time, if it even existed anymore, held no meaning here. The past, the future, even the concept of hope—all were meaningless. He was trapped in a black horizon, where every moment was an eternity, and nothing could ever be the same again.

Floating in the void, Davros glimpsed the fractured remains of what had once been the heart of the galaxy. Where once there had been brilliant stars, there were only dying embers and the faintest glimmers of distant, fading life. The planets that had once teemed with civilization were now lifeless husks, their surfaces burned and scarred, their atmospheres long since shattered. Here and there, in the cold emptiness, the remnants of ships drifted aimlessly, their metal hulls twisted by time and entropy.

The Warp had swallowed the universe whole. And yet, some faint traces of life still clung to existence. As he moved through the wreckage, his perception extended, his senses probing the lifeless debris. And there, among the ashes of all that had been, Davros found them.

Small pockets of survivors—humanity's last remnants—scattered across the void. They floated aimlessly on fragments of broken worlds, clinging to the vestiges of a civilization long lost. Their eyes were empty, vacant, filled with a hollow despair that spoke of lives destroyed, bodies twisted by the Warp's insidious touch, and minds shattered by the horrors they had witnessed. These were no longer people, but husks—empty vessels, devoid of meaning or purpose, drifting in the endless void.

He saw one such group, huddled together on a shard of rock, their ragged clothes barely clinging to their decaying forms. Their eyes locked onto him as he approached, but there was no recognition, no recognition of the man who had once been a god among them. There was only fear—fear of what they saw before them, and fear of what they knew awaited them all.

Uno Nguyen © 2024

"Who... who are you?" one of them whispered, their voice trembling, barely audible over the void's emptiness.

Davros didn't answer immediately. He simply looked at them, his eyes scanning the broken faces of these survivors, the last echoes of humanity. He could see their minds breaking even as he watched, the fragile flickers of life in their eyes giving way to the blackness of despair.

In the distance, he saw the remnants of a once-great city— piles of wreckage, buildings half-collapsed, structures crumbling into dust as if the very laws of reality no longer applied. There had been wars, once—wars that had torn apart the galaxy, leaving behind the husks of civilizations. This was the final battle, the one where humanity had lost everything, and now there was only this: fragments of the past, the memory of what had been.

The survivor continued to stare at Davros, their hollow gaze searching for meaning, for some sign of hope.

"You should've never come here," Davros murmured, his voice barely recognizable. It was a voice stripped of humanity, cold and distant, a mere echo of what had once been a man's soul. He looked at the survivors, the last sparks of humanity in the ruins of everything that had once been.

There was no hope for them. There was no hope for him, either.

As they drew closer, their faces twitching with a mixture of awe and fear, Davros turned, his body shifting unnaturally in the broken reality. He could feel the presence of the Watchers, even if they were not physically there. They had set him on this path, molded him into something unrecognizable, and now there was no turning back.

The survivors reached out to him, but Davros recoiled, not because of fear or revulsion, but because there was nothing left to give them. No answers. No salvation. Not for them, and not for himself.

The universe had died. The galaxy was gone. There was only the void. And in the void, Davros would drift forever, a god in his own mind, but a prisoner of a reality he could no longer comprehend.

The void stretched endlessly, an ocean of nothingness, swallowing the broken remnants of time and space. Davros drifted, caught between realms, between the past and the infinite expanse of empty future. The survivors were like scattered insects on a decaying carcass, struggling to cling to life while the universe they had once known slipped beyond their grasp. They had no place in this darkened world, not anymore.

And neither did he.

But even amidst this eternal emptiness, a flicker of something—something like *purpose*—stirred within him. It was the barest whisper, a faintest tug, but it gnawed at the edges of his mind with a hunger that had not been there before. Davros couldn't understand it, not fully. What could possibly matter in a universe already dead? What was worth striving for in a place where everything, including his own soul, had been stripped away? Yet the pull, strange and unrelenting, persisted.

It was the artifact.

The survivors, broken and ravaged by the void, had spoken of it in hushed tones, their voices quivering as if even mentioning its name could invite the wrath of forces beyond comprehension. The artifact was not just a relic; it was an impossible thing—ancient, powerful, and said to contain the *last hope* for the universe, for *reality itself.*

They had heard stories of it, whispered fragments from the furthest reaches of the galaxy. Some said it had been left behind by beings older than the Gods of Chaos themselves. Others claimed it had been crafted by the Emperor himself before his fall into madness. There were rumors of its existence long before the great destruction—the Necron, the Chaos Gods, the end of everything.

Uno Nguyen © 2024

Now, in this fractured reality, the artifact was the only thing left that might offer salvation—or damnation. Either way, it called to him.

Davros didn't know why, but he couldn't resist.

He pushed past the survivors, whose faces were all the same—pale, broken things. They stared at him with eyes that no longer saw, their vacant expressions betraying the hopelessness that consumed them. None of them moved to stop him, nor did they speak. They were already lost, already in the grasp of the void. Their fates were sealed. Only he, the hollowed-out, incomprehensible being that had once been human, was left to answer the call.

As Davros drew closer, a strange tremor wracked his body. He wasn't sure whether it was from the psychic energy of the artifact itself or the raw hunger he felt inside. It was as if something, something ancient and incomprehensible, was pulling at the very core of his being.

The artifact rested on a pedestal of jagged stone, half-buried in the wreckage of what had once been a magnificent city. Its form was beyond description—neither solid nor liquid, neither light nor dark. It seemed to ripple and bend the fabric of reality around it, its very shape warping in ways that defied the laws of nature. If it had ever been a physical object, it had long since transcended such limitations. Now it was something *else*—something that bled across time itself.

A pulse emanated from the artifact, filling the space around it with an almost unbearable pressure. The survivors nearby flinched, as if the very act of being in its presence threatened to tear them apart. Yet Davros, as if guided by something deeper than his own will, stepped forward, his footfalls echoing in the suffocating silence.

As he reached out to touch the artifact, the moment his fingers brushed against its surface, a wave of psychic energy surged through him, crashing into his mind with the force of a thousand storms. He screamed—but no sound came. The universe itself seemed to collapse inward on him, a maelstrom of visions, truths, and half-formed images that tore through his fractured psyche.

He saw the stars—dying, flickering out one by one as if time itself were being undone. He saw the face of the Emperor, once noble, once filled with hope, now twisted by grief and madness. He saw the creation of the Imperium, and the eventual betrayal, the rise of the Chaos Gods, and the destruction of everything that had once been. He saw a being whose power transcended even that of the gods, a being who had once been humanity's guiding light, only to be consumed by his own creation—the Imperium, built on the bones of the fallen, the twisted remnants of a once-great dream.

But there, in the depths of these visions, there was something more—something *darker*. The truth of the Emperor's vision, or rather, the *corruption* of it. The Emperor, a being of incredible power, had sought to shape the future of mankind, to elevate humanity to a higher state. But his vision had been flawed from the beginning. The artifact—the key to everything—had once been his creation, a failed attempt to transcend the boundaries of mortality. And in that attempt, the Emperor had unleashed something far worse than even the Chaos Gods could comprehend.

The truth struck Davros like a hammer to the chest. The Emperor had been a force of unimaginable power, yes, but he had also been a part of the *cycle* of destruction, a part of the greater pattern that the Watchers had orchestrated. The universe, the stars, the gods—they were all trapped in a never-ending spiral of birth and decay, a game played by powers that dwarfed even the Emperor himself.

"You cannot escape this," the artifact whispered, its voice like the sound of time unraveling. It spoke to Davros in a language older than anything he had ever known—fragments of concepts and knowledge that shattered the very fabric of his understanding. The power he felt was overwhelming, and yet it was not a *blessing*.

It was a curse.

Uno Nguyen © 2024

"I can't undo it," Davros whispered, staring at the artifact as the truth of the universe's destruction washed over him. The visions shattered like glass, each fragment reflecting the death of reality itself. "The universe... is gone."

He staggered backward, his hands trembling as the weight of the knowledge pressed down upon him. There was no hope. No redemption. No future. The cycle would repeat, as it always had. He had always been a part of the game, just another pawn in the hands of forces too vast for any one mind to comprehend.

The survivors looked at him now, their hollow eyes wide with fear. They had sensed it, too. The artifact had revealed its true nature to them as well, and their spirits had been shattered.

For a moment, it seemed as if the entire universe hung in the balance—the dying remnants of humanity, the shattered galaxy, and Davros, alone in his own awareness of the truth. There was nothing left but the pull of the artifact, its whispers promising power, but offering only despair.

The void had no sound, no life, and yet it throbbed with a kind of terrible expectation. It was the place where all things went to die, where the echoes of forgotten stars whispered in the blackened corners of space. There was nothing here but the weight of eternity, pressing down on Davros, suffocating him.

And now, in his hands, the artifact—his salvation or his doom—was no longer a relic or a powerful device. It was a symbol of the absolute collapse of everything. The silence of the void seemed to deepen, as though the universe itself was holding its breath, awaiting the final act in this tragic drama.

Davros stared at the artifact, and it stared back at him with a thousand blinking eyes—eyes that seemed to stretch beyond time, beyond comprehension. Its energy pulsed in his hands, radiating an overwhelming force that seemed to take shape in his mind. It was not just an object, but a nexus of potential—an embodiment of all the choices that had led him to this point.

Uno Nguyen © 2024

The universe had been born from a single spark, and it was dying now, pulled into an inevitable void. And he, Davros, had played his part—whether he had wanted to or not. Each action, each sacrifice, each bloody decision had been a cog in the greater machine. A machine driven by the forces of Chaos, by the Necron, by the Aeldari, by the Watchers in the Dark.

He had become a puppet in a game played by gods and monsters, with no escape and no redemption. All that was left was this—this artifact, which he now realized was *the key* to the end of everything. If he held it long enough, if he used its power, he could rebuild the universe. It could be his creation, molded in his image.

Or he could destroy it all. Annihilate the artifact, erase existence, and ensure that no cycle would ever repeat again.

The weight of the artifact shifted, pulling at his very soul. His mind burned with questions, with the sheer enormity of the choices he was being asked to make. But there was no clear answer. He could feel it—the pressure of infinite possibilities, each choice more terrible than the last. There was no "right" answer. Only endless suffering.

The Necron's cold, mechanized voice broke the silence. "Use the artifact," it intoned, its voice echoing like the crack of a tomb door. "Rebuild the galaxy. The tomb worlds will rise again. Your power will be eternal."

Davros' fingers twitched, the artifact trembling in his grip as the Necron Overlord's words burrowed into his mind. But before he could respond, a voice, sharp and full of malice, spoke from the shadows.

"You are a fool to reject us," the Chaos God, whose presence had always loomed in the background, finally made itself known. The air grew thick with the stench of burning souls and acrid decay. "The universe was made in our image—*my* image. You will serve me, Davros. You will help me rebuild this broken reality. Power beyond imagining awaits you. All that you desire is within your grasp."

Uno Nguyen © 2024

Davros clenched his jaw, the Chaos God's whispers pulling at the ragged edges of his mind, tempting him, offering him control over the ruins of existence.

And yet, there was something else—something that came to him like a cold shiver down his spine. He felt the presence of the Aeldari, too. Their minds were as cold and calculating as the stars themselves.

"You will not be alone in this," the Aeldari whispered, their voices like a thousand blades cutting through the silence. "The path of the Phoenix awaits you. You need only take the first step. Your rebirth will be our rebirth. You can restore all that was lost, and more."

Davros closed his eyes for a moment, trying to push them out, trying to focus on the raw truth of his existence. He felt the weight of the artifact growing heavier in his hands, its energy seeping through his fingers, burrowing into his skin, filling his bones.

But with every word spoken by the Necron, by Chaos, and by the Aeldari, something deeper began to stir within him. A realization that had been growing ever since he first came to this place—the truth that had been hidden from him for so long.

He was not the center of this universe. He was just another player—no different from the millions of others who had suffered through the cycles of destruction and rebirth. His choices had never truly been his own. He had always been a tool—whether for Rubicon, the Watchers, the Necron, or the gods of Chaos. His actions had been meaningless. And now, as he stood on the edge of the abyss, he realized that all of it—the entire universe—had been *meaningless*.

The artifact—the very thing that could remake reality—was merely a trap, just another tool in the hands of beings who cared nothing for the consequences of their actions. The *Watchers*, the gods, they had all used him as they had used countless others. To them, there was no true victory, no true creation. There was only the hunger of the void, the endless need to consume, to tear, to destroy.

And he? He was nothing but another part of the cycle.

With a deep breath, Davros let the truth wash over him, the crushing weight of it all. His life—his existence—had been nothing but a shadow in the darkness, a fleeting moment of pain and suffering that meant nothing in the grand scope of the cosmos.

The voices of the gods, of the Necron, of the Aeldari, fell silent. They knew. They *felt* it. And for the first time in his life, Davros felt the absence of their influence.

He took a step back, his hands trembling as the artifact pulsed in his grip. He could feel its power—its promise of everything he could ever want. And yet, as it grew stronger, his soul grew colder.

This was the end. The *real* end.

Davros whispered, "I am nothing."

His fingers twitched again, and the artifact cracked—a single, jagged fracture splitting through its core. The very fabric of the universe seemed to buckle under the weight of the decision, a ripple running through reality itself.

The artifact splintered, its energy surging outward, breaking apart as the cycle of existence began to crumble.

"No..." Davros whispered as he watched the artifact unravel, its power cascading outward, taking with it all of his hopes, all of his desires, and every possibility of redemption. The void, once empty and silent, now seemed to *shudder* with the finality of everything.

And as the fabric of the universe began to tear apart at the seams, Davros realized the terrible truth: *nothing*—not the universe, not the gods, not his choices—had ever mattered. There was no creation. There was no destruction. There was only the void.

Uno Nguyen © 2024

And in the void, nothing would ever come again.

The pulse from the shattered artifact rippled through the galaxy like the last heartbeat of a dying star. It traveled far and wide, crossing the empty void with terrifying speed. The last remnants of existence trembled at its touch—galaxies quivered, and the fabric of space and time unraveled at its core. This was the final act, the ultimate destruction of everything.

Davros felt it, the energy radiating through him as though it were part of his very soul. The Warp itself groaned in agony, its countless dimensions flickering and tearing apart, consumed by the immense force of his decision. The stars dimmed, the planets crumbled, and the cosmic balance that had once held all things together was obliterated.

Through the rift of the universe, he watched.

The survivors—those pitiful remnants of humanity who had clung to life in the dying corners of the galaxy—vanished in an instant, reduced to nothing but dust, their cries snuffed out by the void. They were never meant to survive. Not in this universe. Not in the end.

The Necrons, those ancient beings of cold, merciless metal, fell apart like brittle statues. Their eternal empire shattered, their metallic forms crumbling to ash. The silent tomb worlds that had once sprawled across the galaxy now lay abandoned, forgotten in the wake of their masters' collapse. The Necron Overlords—who had once stood as titans, immutable and eternal—were no more. They, too, had been caught in the riptide of this final destruction.

The Tyranids—those ravenous horrors from the void—had devoured everything in their path, their hunger endless, their needs insatiable. But now, even they were consumed by their own insatiable nature. Their swarms froze, frozen in place by the overwhelming force of the collapse. Their hunger, once all-encompassing, turned inwards. The Tyranids, like everything else, had become an empty void. They were as hungry as they were lost.

Uno Nguyen © 2024

Even the Warp itself—the very heart of chaos—began to disintegrate, its layers of reality peeling away like old skin. The Chaos Gods, those entities of ancient malice, trembled. Their thrones, once powerful and unshakable, now splintered like brittle stone. The Warp trembled in agony, its energies imploding, collapsing under the weight of the universe's true emptiness. Nothing remained untouched. Nothing remained.

Davros was alone. The last thing left.

His body, now a grotesque, unrecognizable mockery of his former self, floated through the decaying cosmos. He had once been a man. He had once held power over life and death, created empires and destroyed worlds. He had walked among the stars, wielding the forces of science and madness as if they were his to command. But now, he was nothing more than a thing of broken flesh and twisted steel, a twisted echo of what he once was.

He had become the embodiment of the end. The void itself.

His form, once human, now warped and stretched beyond recognition, was no longer bound by the rules of the physical universe. Time and space held no sway over him. He drifted in an endless ocean of emptiness, a silent witness to the collapse of all things.

His hands, once stained with the blood of millions, now drifted in the vast silence. There was no longer a galaxy to conquer, no stars to burn, no people to enslave. There was only the nothingness. The cold, empty void that stretched infinitely in all directions. There was no sound here. No warmth. No light.

It is finished, he thought. But even his thoughts felt distant, fractured, and unreal.

He floated aimlessly, the weight of everything—or nothing— pressing in on him. The endless silence surrounded him, unbroken. There was no escape, no hope, no salvation. The universe had passed beyond the point of no return, and all the forces that had once driven

Uno Nguyen © 2024

it—the gods, the powers, the mortals—were gone. There was no longer any purpose to anything. It had all been an illusion.

And now, the only truth that remained was this:

The end.

The pulse of the artifact had spread across the fabric of all existence, undoing everything. It was the final death knell, the last breath of a universe that had long since lost its meaning. The last remnants of time and space melted away, becoming nothing more than fleeting memories. Every moment, every scream, every heartbeat that had once defined existence was gone, swallowed by the abyss.

Davros looked out into the endless horizon—an expanse of infinite darkness, stretched forever in all directions. There was nothing. No light. No sound. No movement. Only the cold, unyielding void.

He had done this. He had ended it all. There was no turning back. There was nothing left to fight for.

He felt the weight of that truth press down on him, a crushing force that left him gasping for breath—though he did not need to breathe anymore. There was no air in the void. There was only... nothing.

I have destroyed it all, Davros thought. *And yet... I am still here.*

The thought echoed in his mind, growing louder and louder. The irony of it—he, the one who had sought to remake the universe, was now the last thing left. He was the embodiment of its end, the final witness to its final destruction.

Davros closed his eyes. There was no reason to continue. No reason to fight.

There was only the end.

He whispered it, his voice barely a sound in the void.

"The end. The only truth."

And then, with nothing left but silence, he ceased to be.

The universe was no more.

Davros stood in the middle of nothingness, the absolute absence of existence. Time, which had once moved in a relentless march from moment to moment, was gone. The forward momentum of reality had been swallowed whole by the emptiness. There were no stars to blink out, no worlds to burn, no galaxies to collapse. There was no sound. No heat. No light. Only a boundless, crushing, infinite void that stretched beyond comprehension.

Even the remnants of his once-broken body had faded, like dust carried on a wind that no longer blew.

There was nothing to anchor him, nothing to hold his consciousness together. His eyes—if he could still call them eyes—saw only the infinite blackness that swallowed all things. His thoughts, those fragile remnants of humanity, fractured like shattered glass. He was adrift, but even that notion felt absurd in a place where there was nothing to drift *through*. No more "space" existed to contain him, no more "time" to measure him.

The Watchers, the Chaos Gods, the Necron Lords, the Tyranids, the Aeldari, and even the smallest of humans—every last one was gone. The billions of minds that had once populated the galaxy were erased. Their suffering, their pain, their joy, their betrayals—all of it had evaporated into nothingness, as though it had never been.

And yet Davros remained.

He had destroyed everything—*everything*—but he could not escape the consequences of his own actions. He had sought power, immortality, control over the fabric of the universe itself. He had become the embodiment of that destruction. But even in that, he found no solace, no satisfaction.

The void stretched on, empty and indifferent to his existence. The weight of absolute emptiness pressed on him from all sides. It was not the void of space, not the cold and quiet absence between stars. It was far more profound—far deeper. It was an absence that transcended all things. It was *nothing*. Pure and complete.

In the silence, Davros felt something stir within him—a distant, hollow sensation of something that once had been. A memory of life. A flicker of a time when he was *alive*.

Was this what he had wanted? To be the last thing in existence? To outlast even the gods, to break the wheel of the universe?

I am... he thought, but the thought itself dissolved before it could fully form.

Nothing remained to contradict him. No laws of reality to prevent it. He was nothing. And yet... he was still there. A disembodied thought. A broken remnant of consciousness, without a body to house it, without a mind to support it.

There was nothing left to burn. No world to conquer. No life to destroy.

His scream, the last vestige of sound in the universe, was swallowed by the void before it could echo back. It was absorbed into the infinite expanse, lost to time that no longer flowed. There was no longer a beginning or an end. No before, no after. Only an infinite, timeless now.

He had no more enemies, no more allies. There was no war to fight. No need to struggle.

There was only silence.

And then—nothing. No thoughts. No awareness. No Davros.

THE END

Made in United States
Troutdale, OR
01/06/2025

27611681R00063